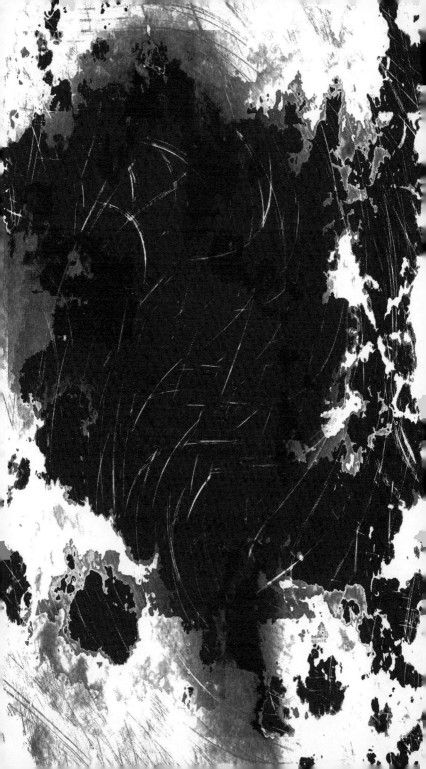

OVERSIGHT

by Michael Bailey

Published by Written Backwards
www.nettirw.com

First Paperback Edition
ISBN: 978-1-7327244-5-7

for
Meghan Arcuri
Paul Michael Anderson
Erinn L. Kemper

Long Fiction

Short Fiction

OVERSIGHT

"Walking with a friend in the dark is better than walking alone in the light."

– Helen Keller

"The most important kind of freedom is to be what you really are. You trade your reality for a role. You give up your ability to feel, and in exchange, put on a mask."

– Jim Morrison

"The world only exists in your eyes. You can make it as big or as small as you like."

– F. Scott Fitzgerald

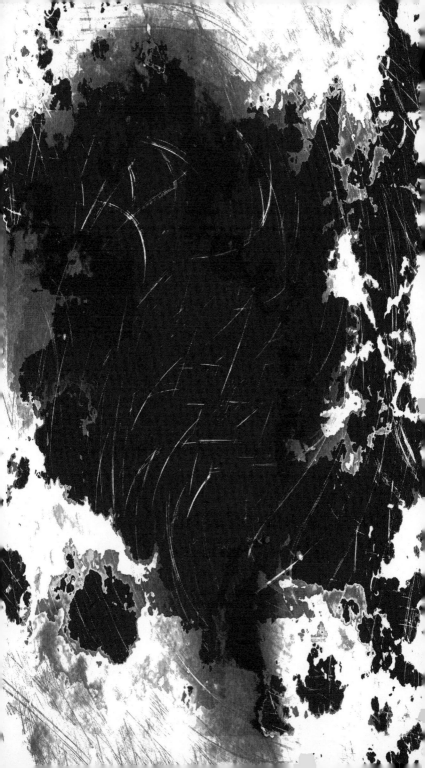

DARKROOM

"You're really going with me," Grace said, not as a question, and tied a bandana to cover her sister's eyes. She made the knot tight, centered it behind her head.

"I can see through the material," Alice said.

"You're supposed to be able to see through the material. A little or a lot?"

"A little. Shapes of things, mostly. I see a silhouette of you, and can tell you're wearing a bandana, too, but I can't make out your face. You look, I don't know, *undeveloped*."

Grace thought the reference was clever, as she'd had much experience developing film in the darkroom she had made out of her basement. The ground-level windows had been blacked out with paint, and the one bulb dangling from the ceiling was amber and only used while developing film. Grace had no use for light otherwise.

"Is this how you see the world?" Alice asked.

Under her own bandana—one Alice said was white skulls over black—Grace's eyes were covered with gauze, taped to her face. She'd lived sightless for the most part, wearing the bandana in public and toting a cane for the blind so as not to frighten anyone. Grace's eyes wanted nothing to do with the world. She'd rather *not* see. Only in the dark-room would she take off their coverings, only while developing.

"Sort of," Grace said. "In the light everything's lost in red-hued black, and in the dark everything's simply … gone."

In the dark, we all look the same, she thought, and this pleased her.

"Where are we going, anyway? I mean, *when* are we going?"

"2004."

"We were what, seven and eight?"

"Nine and ten, and Dad was thirty-four," Grace said, knowing the math.

Ten had been such a bad year, or so she remembered.

"How did we get so old? And so fast?"

Their dad would have been ninety-four if he were still alive, but he had died from a hemorrhagic stroke. She needed her little sister with her this time, to *not* see, to *not* hear, but to be there for moral support; even now, seventy years old, she needed her.

"You'll wear this too," Grace said, feeling for the headphones. They were noise cancelling, and she found and placed them over her sister's ears.

"Can you hear me?" she said. "Alice! Can you hear me?" she said louder, and so she temporarily removed them and said, "Nothing?"

"Nothing what?"

"You couldn't hear me," Grace said, again not a question. "Good."

"How will we get around, without sight and without sound?"

"You remember the house as much as I do. All I have to do is remember what I want to remember, a certain *time*, a certain *place*, and that's where we'll go now, where I'll take you, *to* that time. Remember Mom and Dad's bedroom, the nightstand where Dad used to keep his pile of books? How he used to read three or four at any given time? We're going to shift into their bedroom, next to that nightstand. The year the furnace in the attic broke and we used space heaters next to our beds. It doesn't have to be an *exact* date and time, just an approximation of when and where. A memory. That's where we're going, to the winter of 2004, and we're going to take Dad's picture while he's sleeping."

For sixty days Grace had traveled blindly to the

past. She'd found a way to *shift*, to be there without actually being there, and she was getting better at it every day, even without her sight, the meditations easier to slip into, and with each shift she could further travel through years that had seemingly taken forever to pass.

Grace held an old camera, a Nikon Nikkormat FTN 35mm, even though her sister couldn't see it. "We're going to take Dad's picture," she said again.

"Like the ones in the book?"

"Yes, while he's still asleep, in the early morning, a time light enough for the picture to turn out."

Before adorning the blindfolds, Grace had pushed a book across the table to her sister—a stack of photos bound together at the spine by a metal clasp. Inside were a collection of fifty-nine eight-by-ten black-and-white photographs of their father, each taken from a different year, starting with 2064 and stepping backward through time, the earliest dated 2005. Each photo was of her father in bed, early in the morning before rising, and each photo had been taken on a different day over the last two months to cover a particular year. The idea was for Dad to age in reverse as you flipped from first page to last. He'd always slept in the same position, on his back, which is why he often snored, and why Grace knew the photos would be similar, despite his reverse aging.

"You've never seen these," Alice had said.

"I don't want to see them until I'm finished."

"And when will that be?"

"When I can't remember enough of Dad to go back, I guess."

Grace could remember as far back as kindergarten, but not much farther than that. She would be ten years old this time, in 2004, so maybe only five or six more photos of her father at most before she'd consider the book complete.

The photos of Dad sleeping were the only ones Grace had shown to Alice so far, and this time around she'd take the one of him sleeping and add it to the back of the book, and use the rest of the Fuji film to document home as she and her sister sightlessly and soundlessly moved from room to room. They were raised in that home and their father had died there, so she knew the house inside and out, could roam around and snap photographs at will, despite lacking two of her senses. And this would be her sixtieth day doing it blindly.

Grace had taken entire rolls worth of photographs of the past, and each time she'd start with one of her father asleep in bed—that way she'd always know the first shot developed was the one to add to the reverse-aging book—and then she'd take as many photos as her budget would allow, each day a focus on a different year. She'd gone back to her past often, not only in the early morning hours, but *all* hours.

The darkroom housed stacks of photographs, filed in boxes prearranged by year: 2063, 2062, 2061, all the way back to 2005. There were perhaps thousands upon thousands of black-and-white photographs. Later they could develop the photos from 2004 together, in the darkroom, and then maybe she'd start looking through them, *really* looking through them—no longer concerned about contrast or quality, the way film developers never truly care about anything but the process. Then maybe she'd look through photos from the other years, having Alice there with her for support. The last sixty days had been spent shooting and developing sixty years of the past, not necessarily reliving what she'd captured along the way.

She wanted Alice to understand how the process worked before she'd allow her sister to become more involved, before Grace would even consider removing the coverings permanently from her eyes in order to see what she'd accomplished blindly these last two months. She was too afraid to go at it alone. There were too many unknowns. Too many frightening senses in the past she'd perhaps never come to understand, hence the precautions. The entire process of shifting back through time was so utterly *strange*.

Grace could take things with her, she'd learned through experimentation, physical things: the blindfold, the headphones, her camera, and hopefully now even her sister.

"So we'll be blind, basically, and deaf because of the headphones," Alice said.

"I'll be right next to you," Grace said. "We can lock elbows."

"What happens if we wake Dad, or Mom?"

"They won't be able to see us or hear us because we aren't really there. They won't be able to hear the camera, because the camera's not really there. And *no*, they won't be able to run into us either, if it comes to that, or feel us. You have to remember that where we're going is in the past. We're not really *there*. We're on another plane entirely. At least I think that's how it works. It's all so confusing to me."

"I'll believe it when I see it. The photographs, I mean."

Alice, Grace knew, had only agreed to go with her this time because of the photobook of their father sleeping, the captured memories too real and too precise to have been modified by computer program. Flipping through the book would be like watching him struggle in his sleep, Grace imagined, every little twitch sending him another year younger.

"What happens if I lose a shoe? What if—"

"You'll be fine."

Grace had tried leaving items in the past as well—anything she touched during the shift could be taken with her, hypothetically: a pencil, a note to her mother, and on another occasion, a hand-written note to her younger self to see if she'd remember the words as her older self, but when-ever she shifted back, the items would still be with her, as if they'd never left the present. *Remember Google*, one note had read. *When you're old enough, buy stock in Google, as much as you can*, and of course when she returned she remembered the words, but only because she'd written them down moments before going back; her bank account unchanged, the handwritten note not left in the past but on the floor next to her, even though she'd placed it on her bedside table in her existence as a thirteen-year-old before shifting back to the present.

She'd also tried taking items *from* the past, physical items, but they always stayed where they belonged, in their own time, in their own plane of existence.

You can't change the past; you can only take it with you, she thought, the *it* in this case meaning memories. *You can only change outcomes of the future.*

Why could she bring physical things with her to the past? She wondered this often. Perhaps because these things were not yet memories. Perhaps—

"Bring something with you, something you can break, or something you can alter." She knew her sister well, knew she'd want to experiment as Grace first had.

Behind the blindfold, behind her gauze-covered eyes, Grace could see nothing, and imagined her sister, also blindfolded, searching around the room with her hands. She heard Alice take something from the table.

"A piece of paper," Alice said. 'I'll tear it in half when we get there, and I'll try to leave half there and bring the other half back."

Grace smiled, knowing what would happen: nothing. She'd return with two torn halves of a piece of paper.

The camera could break the rules, she'd discovered after trial by error. Perhaps it had something to do with the film, the fact it would remain undeveloped until she returned. Grace could use the old Nikon to snap photos, could develop the film in the basement by feel alone, if she'd wanted to— or *needed* to—could see the captured past through these photographs after their final water rinse and hanging them up to dry. *If* she wanted to see them.

She'd tried a Polaroid months before blinding herself and using the Nikon, snapping pictures from her past and letting them develop there, directly from the camera—and they *had*—yet when she'd return the snapshots they were the same fuzzy black of her blinded sight, as if she'd never taken them, despite that the camera had spit them out. She'd attempted snapping a shot with the Polaroid and shifting back *before* the film had developed, but the results were the same. Grace tried digital as well, but those shots returned fuzzy-black, albeit sequentially numbered by date / time on the memory card and taking up space, and she couldn't help but wonder why; something had to be hiding in the pixels, otherwise each file would be 0K and unreadable by both the camera and her laptop. Only black-and-white film seemed to do the trick.

The Nikon had belonged to her father, one of the few things Grace had kept after he died; perhaps that's why it was able to capture the past.

"Why do we even need the blindfolds, or the headphones?" Alice asked.

"It's the only way this works," Grace said, not wanting to scare her with what she already knew. "I'm sure there's something paradoxical about seeing one's past while still existing in one's present, or seeing one's earlier self."

"I haven't thought of that. Seeing us when we're younger. I mean, I've seen pictures of us when we were younger, but to *be* there, to take those pictures, to take our own pictures of *us* ... I can't believe you've never looked at those photos of Dad."

The first time she'd successfully shifted to the past, Grace had seen things moving in the dark, impossible shadows, black shapes teasing her peripherals. And there were sounds.

"I stopped wanting to see Dad a long time ago," Grace said, killing the moment. "Okay, put on the headphones and breathe deeply, in and out. Think about the winter of 2004 and only think of that, and if this works like it always has, we'll shift there."

"I don't like that word: *shift.*"

"It's the only word that seems to fit."

"How long does it take?" Alice asked.

"Not long, maybe a couple minutes at most. I'll hold your hand and will squeeze twice when I know we're there, and then we'll lock arms. We'll start with the picture of Dad, and then Mom. And we'll go from there."

She asked after a moment if Alice had put on the noise-cancelling headphones, but she didn't answer, and so she put on her own.

Grace thought of her parents' bedroom as she'd remembered it sixty years ago, when her father was thirty-four and she and Alice were nine and ten, when they'd both get scared from night noises and together they'd walk down the hall, hand-in-hand, knocking ever so softly against their parents' bedroom door. She thought of Mom and Dad—*never Dad and Mom for some reason*—sleeping in the early hours of the morning, even though she couldn't see them, the sun beginning to rise, its light permeating through the open-curtained window. She thought of her father's snoring, the repetitive sawing, and even though her ears were now covered, she could somehow hear him in her mind, as though hearing him through the bedroom door all those years ago, waiting to be let inside. She thought of Alice next to her, walking through the door, hand-in-hand, the two of them watching over their parents while they slept: Mom on the left, Mad on the right. *Mom*, one of them would so often say, *can we sleep with you?* but they wouldn't wake their parents this time because they weren't really there; the Grace and Alice of 2004 were sleeping sound in their beds in the shared room down the hall. She could feel Alice standing with her now, not as a child, but as a sixty-nine-year-old adult woman.

Alice squeezed Grace's hand, twice, instead of the other way around. She knew they were there, in the past. Grace squeezed back, twice, and then locked arms so she could hold the camera in front of her.

She imagined Alice could see darkened silhouettes of her parents on the bed, as she had the first few times she'd shifted before double-blinding herself, remembering the cloudy outlines under the blankets and head-like shapes on the pillows.

Behind the gauze, behind the bandana, Grace opened her eyes, knowing exactly where her father would be, even though she couldn't see a thing.

Undeveloped.

Grace held the Nikon in front of her, wound the roll of film, and raised the camera, chest level, pointing the lens. The bedspread would be white, she knew, their parents covered like corpses in a morgue, the early morning light making the mostly empty room look much like a black-and-white photograph.

Because she'd imagined herself—and Alice—next to her father's side of the bed, as she always had, looking over him, that is where she and her sister had shifted, she knew, and so she took a photo of their father sleeping, and counted *one*.

She wound the camera, took the next photo of her mother, counted *two*.

Twenty-two remaining on the roll.

Alice pulled her in close. Even with the bandana, perhaps she'd seen unknown shapes moving about, the camera flashes like lightning over their covered parents, black tendrils creeping in corners and giving the dead room life.

Grace felt a chill on her back and she and her sister spun in unison.

Flash.

Three, she counted, taking a picture of the room behind them.

I don't like this, she imagined her sister saying into the dark. *I don't like this.*

They moved around the room in silence, all but for the soft drone of the noise-cancelling headphones. And they moved around in darkness, all but for the strobes of light provided by the camera every time she took a picture.

Four, five, Grace counted as they continued down the hall, winding the camera between shots. *Six.* Along the walls would be multi-photo picture frames. A few of the photos she took would be of older photos. *New pictures of old pictures,* she marveled, *but somehow not nearly as time-distant as they should be.* She could almost feel the shag carpet beneath her feet as they moved along. Halfway to their room, Grace reached to her left for what should be the bathroom door, but it either wasn't there or was wide open; she stopped long enough to take a picture of what she remembered would be a combination mirror and medicine cabinet, wondering if the photo would capture their reflections, or the reflections of something worse. *Seven.*

At the end of the hall she took another, counted *eight,* which she knew would be their closed bedroom door. Sixty years ago, the door would have had a hand-drawn KEEP OUT sign with Crayoned flowers sprouting from the edges.

Alice pulled her in close, and Grace imagined she was thinking *No!* to not go in there, to not take photos of the two of them sleeping. Alice pulled against her arm, to turn her back so they could instead go into the kitchen or the living room, but Grace forced her like any daring sister would, and together they faced the closed door for a long moment, taking deep breaths.

I don't want to do this, her sister would say, or *could*

be saying for all she knew. Grace reached for the doorknob and turned it, and for the briefest of heartbeats, she felt the brush of two fingers over the back of her hand, but then the sensation was gone. Perhaps Alice trying to stop her one last time, or perhaps one of the slithering shadows passing over her skin, and then she opened the door.

Grace remembered the squeak, now muted by the headphones, how it had sounded whenever she'd sneak out of her room before tiptoeing down the hall to peer around the corner of the living room to spy on her parents. Sometimes she'd catch them eating ice cream, or watching television. Sometimes they'd let her join in for a minute. Sometimes they'd tell her it was *way* past her bedtime and send her back down the hall.

Flash.

Nine, like her sister saying no in German. *Let's go back, Grace. I really don't want to do this anymore please can we go back please let's go back!*

Arm linked to arm, Grace pulled her hesitant sister into the room of their childhood. On the left would be Alice's bed, *ten*, and on the right her own identical bed, *eleven*, the room split evenly down the middle by blue tape because they'd always argued about sides and measurements and tape was the only compromise to make it truly even. Grace wound the Nikon, snapped a shot down the center of the room, counted *twelve*. She hoped the line would split the photo evenly, the sole window in the room directly in the center.

Half the roll remaining.

She felt her sister stir, in a way that Grace could only assume Alice had torn the paper she'd taken with her in two, and had tossed one half. Grace pointed the camera to the floor, counted *thirteen* as she felt the shutter of the camera taking another picture. She imagined the torn paper on the left side of the room as she wound the camera.

They turned out of the room, neither liking their backs to the empty hall. Grace imagined the door squeaking closed, and then felt a quick vibration at her feet and a breeze at her back, as if someone had slammed the door shut from the other side, a sensation startling her trigger-happy finger to take a shot of the floor.

That was you, wasn't it? Alice would ask, knowing Grace had reached for the door as well, just as she had, to make sure the door had closed on its own.

Not on its own.

She let go of the camera long enough to squeeze Alice's arm, to let her know everything was okay, to let her know they were almost done.

Fourteen, she told herself. *Ten shots left.*

She and her sister tiptoed down the hall to the living room, and in doing so, brought back memories of late-night Klondike bars and the buttery smell of popcorn and watching movies on the couch and, of course, the spying they'd sometimes do on their parents, sometimes one of them venturing out for reconnaissance, sometimes both.

Ten silent steps, which so long ago used to be twenty.

At the entrance to the living room, Grace panned the camera blindly across the room, taking shots and winding: *fifteen, sixteen, seventeen*, she counted.

She ran her free hand across the wall, to give her a sense of where she was in the room, her fingers tracing wallpaper textured much like leathery skin. She took a picture of the front entryway: *eighteen*; she took a picture leading into the kitchen: *nineteen*. She guided Alice with their baby-slide-steps across the carpet until their feet found linoleum. Flash: *twenty*. Flash: *twenty-one*.

A cold breeze at their backs sent them spinning, their arms untangling for the briefest of moments. She imagined her sister flailing in the dark, reaching for her, as Grace was doing the same, and then their arms found each other.

What happens if I lose her before shifting back?

She'd return with her to the present, she assured herself. Everything always had.

Flash: *twenty-two*, she counted, a selfie from as far out as she could reach.

The sudden brightness, she wondered, *why hadn't it startled Alice?*

Those arms lead her back through the living

room the way they'd come as Grace wound the film in the camera, nearly running, Alice leading *her* this time, through the hallway, tripping over something—*twenty-three*, an accidental shot of their feet—and hastily making their way to their parents' bedroom once again.

Grace imagined they were standing where they'd started, looking over Dad. She imagined her sister softly chanting *let's go back let's go back please let's go back* and so she took the final shot, *twenty-four*, and shifted them back to the present.

"I don't ever want to do that again!" Alice said, loud enough to be heard through the noise-cancelling headphones as their arms unlinked, and then in a softer voice as both sets of headphones clunked against the table in front of them, "Don't you *ever* make me do that again. We were *really* there, weren't we? 2004. We were really there."

"We were," Grace said, "as much as we could."

She knew her sister had more questions, but also knew she was too afraid to ask—questions she'd asked herself the first time she'd shifted alone. She understood this by the sounds: Alice's rapid breaths, her sister slamming the bandana hard against the table.

"Don't ever make me do that again," Alice said in a softer voice.

"You don't have to, unless you want to."

"I kind of do. Go back, I mean."

She remembered how she'd felt after returning that first time: the adrenaline rush, the pounding of her heart, the impossibility of not breathing without thinking about breathing, the thought of all the things you couldn't hear and the things you couldn't see, and how vividly they stuck with you.

"The paper's still here," Alice said. "Torn in half, but still here. I ripped the paper outside our bedroom door and tossed half to the floor. I kept the other half wadded in my hand. And it's still *here*, in my hand. The other half is on the floor."

"But you remember the sensation of walking. Through the house, I mean."

"We were *there*," Alice said.

"We were," Grace said, smiling, and she could feel her sister smiling, too.

"How do we know I didn't simply tear the paper here, in the present?"

"I guess we don't. And I guess you did."

How funny would it be for someone to walk in on them while shifted? Two older women sitting next to each other on a couch in front of a coffee table, arms interlinked, eyes covered with bandanas, both wearing headphones, as if experiencing some sort of horrific virtual reality game without proper equipment.

Grace wound the film in the camera to the end of the roll and popped off the back cover of the camera. She pinched the roll of Fuji film between her index finger and thumb and removed her bandana. The room lightened with only the gauze taped over her eyes. She probably wasn't the most pleasant person to look at, she knew, like someone who'd recently recovered from Lasik, not yet ready to remove the bandages to see the world anew.

"Want to see?" Grace asked.

"What, *now?*"

"Of course now. Let's process these downstairs and you can take a look."

"Why don't you take those things off?" Alice said, a question but not really a question. "You look ridiculous," she said, the voice nearer.

She felt her sister's fingers at her face and batted them away.

"Not until we're in the darkroom."

"What are you afraid of?"

You wouldn't understand, Grace thought. She'd only ever taken off the gauze while in the darkroom, and only after she'd made sure the room was as dark as it could be.

She led her sister to the basement. The blind leading the sighted as her fingers traced the walls of the hallway, as they had following so many previous shifts, until they reached the door to the basement, which was ajar. Grace flipped the switch for the amber light, for Alice's sake, and together they walked down the stairs, Grace guided by the handrail.

"My word!" Alice said, apparently taking in the room. "You've been busy."

Grace had lined the boxes against the wall so they wouldn't be in the way, each filled with photographs from their labeled years. Sixty boxes, the last of which was empty.

Alice slipped and nearly took Grace down the stairs with her, but Grace kept them upright and asked if she was all right.

"I'm still shaky from before, but I'm okay."

"Can you shut the door behind us?" she asked, and waited until she heard it. Even with the door closed, she knew there'd be white light leaking through its edges, and so they made their way down the stairs and around the corner where light would be most absent.

Another five steps and they were at the developing station.

"You really do look ridiculous," Alice said.

Grace held her hands outward like a tired zombie until they met the table, where she'd setup a makeshift table and sink with a *wet* area on the left and a *dry* area on the right. Only there did she take off the gauze bandages covering her eyes. The darkroom glowed deep amber as her eyes adjusted to the yellow light. Even the smallest of illuminations was difficult to let in.

Above the wet area was a light-proof extraction fan to keep the room properly ventilated for chemical fumes—with ductwork leading outside—which was much like a range-hood extraction over an oven. The *dry* area had the Bessler enlarger with a 35mm Nikon lens, a timer, as well as sealed photographic paper, unused developer tanks, folded towels, and a few sets of tongs. On a shelf below were various chemicals. She'd installed a water filter under the sink after the first few photographs she'd developed were tainted by sediment. To the right of the station ran three wires strung all the way to the far most wall, with clips to hang photos so they could dry over water runnels. It was quite the setup.

Alice watched her through the various steps of exposing the film, the enlargement, and then the print processing.

"I want to watch all of these develop," Grace said, placing the first image into the stop bath. The first, her unfinished father, stared up at her, sleeping in a 1.5% solution of acetic acid.

"Yeah?"

"I think I'm ready for that, with you here."

Even after so much experience developing film these last two months, it still took procedural time for each picture: three minutes with constant agitation in a developer solution of 50/50 Dektol and water to bring out the image, thirty seconds rocking her sleeping father in a solution of acetic acid to stop the development, another sixty seconds in a fixer solution of sodium thiosulfate to make the photographic image insensitive to light, a few minutes holding Dad under a tap water rinse, ten minutes in an Zonal Pro archival rinse, and finally moving him into a water holding bath until the other twenty-three images were there with him, at which time she'd give each of the twenty-four photographs their final wash and hang them to dry.

"It's really Dad," Alice said, staring into the water, "Dad from 2004."

"He's half as old as we are now," Grace said.

They stood silently for a while, Grace holding her father's image by a small set of tongs. He lay in bed, mouth open, caught amidst a snore, mid-sleep. If anything, he looked *fake* asleep, like when she and her sister would pretend to sleep when he'd check on them.

"He looks like he does in the others," Alice said, "from the book, only younger."

She decided not to leave this one in the holding bath, and gave it its final wash, hanging the black-and-white picture of Dad from a clip on the wires.

Twenty-three remaining, Grace thought, assigning each a number.

> 1. Their father sleeping in the early hours of the morning, or pretending to sleep, his body under the covers, head tilted back on his pillow, mouth open. Mom's hand in the frame, reach-

35

ing to him. The rest of the bed out of
focus, dark clouds of black around the
edges, as if from underexposure.

They repeated the steps for each of the photos
they'd taken. Developer / stop / fixer / water rinse
/ archival rinse. They didn't spend much time *looking* at the photos, but simply making sure they were
processed correctly. *I don't know if this one turned out
okay*, Alice would say now and then, or *Does this
look right to you?* or *What's this black smudge?* she'd
say, thinking she'd done something wrong. They
took turns moving the images from one tray to the
next, through the rinses, and stacked each in the
tray marked ARCHIVAL RINSE until the rest of them
were ready for their final rinse and could be hung
to dry. They were careful with every photograph,
handling them from the corners with tongs, and
clipping each onto the wires where they could drip
to the floor in the dark amber light.

2. Their mother sleeping, or pretending, her body under the covers, head
tilted away from their father, mouth
closed. A silver or gold necklace. She
was beautiful, even in slumber. Dad,
next to her, streaked in black smudges,
as if fingers of a giant hand held him
down.

DARKROOM

"My first attempt," Alice said, "I dropped the tongs in the tray while you were rinsing the picture of Dad. The tongs went under the photo so I tweezed out the paper with my fingers. How old was Mom in this one?"

"Thirty-one, three years younger—which tray?"

"Oh yeah," she said, and then, "the second one."

"Did you wash your hands? It's acetic acid, only 1.5%, but you should still wash your hands. Treat this like a clean room."

Alice washed her hands while Grace clipped the next photograph. She remembered this one by its blurriness. She'd felt a coldness behind them after taking the two photos of their parents—which they'd both felt as they pivoted, the photo taken mid-turn.

> 3. Like the Edvard Munch painting, *The Scream*, their father's sleeping form stretches impossibly, as if he too were painted in oils and pastels, those giant fingers from before pulling him apart, filling the photograph with his agony. His eyes, terribly white, stretch like imperfect pearls. Mouth caught in a scream.

> 4. An empty hallway, a door in the distance.

5. The same hallway, focused on the wall with multi-photo picture frames: four-year-old Alice in a bathing suit, holding a pale of sand, a plastic shovel; five-year-old Grace standing next to her with a too-heavy bucket of water; a family portrait from K-mart with a fake spring background; other picture frames line the wall, out of focus. The door to their bathroom, farther down the hall and to the left, open like a maw and seeping darkness over shag carpet.

6. The same hallway, focused on the right wall, with more picture-framed photographs: Mom and Dad—*always Mom and Dad and never the other way around*—on their wedding day. Mom wearing a white dress and Dad wearing a black suit and bowtie; Uncle James holding a version of Grace still in diapers; a black lab they'd adopted named Charlie; other picture frames line the wall, out of focus.

New pictures of old pictures, Grace thought again, *but somehow not nearly as time-distant as they should be.*

7. A round flash of light from the camera, reflected from the bathroom mirror / medicine cabinet. In the darkness, behind and between the points of the blinding star-like flash: seventy-year-old Grace and sixty-nine-year-old Alice, both blindfolded, the black around them seemingly trying to swallow them whole; reflections of their older selves.

"This proves we were there!" Alice said, standing next to her. "I mean, I know we were there, because we were *there*, but this is *proof!* What's that behind you?"

Behind Grace, in the photo, was a blurry, eyeless, demonic face, something a child would draw with a black crayon while angry; albeit the face was completely out of focus and not a face at all, but shadows contorted by the reflection of the camera flash in the mirror, or from the corner of one of the multi-photo picture frames behind them.

"I don't think it's anything," Grace said, although she remembered a feeling of having some*one* or some*thing* following them down the hall. Some*one* or some*thing* cold.

8. The end of the hall. The door to their bedroom, cracked open, with a

sign taped to the front reading KEEP
OUT in childish handwriting, Crayoned
flowers sprouting from the edges.

This photo seemed like a warning to not go on.

"I'm not sure I want to do this anymore," her
sister said, just as she'd imagined Alice saying
before they'd opened the door to their childhood
bedroom.

The brush of two fingers over the back of her hand.

The amber bulb above them flickered.

*Let's go back, Grace. I really don't want to do this
anymore please can we go back please let's go back!*

But Grace had opened the door anyway.

9. A toy-cluttered room they'd shared
as children, on the left Alice's bed, and
on the right Grace's. A line of tape
splits the room in two, leading from
the door to window. They'd again
captured their reflections in the glass,
the flash of camera dull from the
distance and creating an effect of a
third person—*a child made of darkness
and light*—standing between them,
their old interlocked arms and the
absence of light between them creating arms and legs. To the far left: half
of Alice under the covers; to far right:

a mass of blankets and stuffed animals
covering half a child-like mound.

"Who—?" Alice started to ask, but Grace had
hung two more pictures to dry.

10. Alice's side of the room. Alice in
bed, not sleeping. Alice sitting upright,
staring wide-eyed straight ahead, her
body a perfect ninety degree angle.

11. Grace's side of the room. Grace's
bed empty save for a mess of plush
animals and a disrupted pillow.

"Where *am* I?" Grace asked, just as Alice asked,
"Where *are* you?"

12. The same shot as #9, but with
reflected older versions of them gone,
the third child of darkness and light
gone, the window black. Tape down
the center of the room, creating a
mirrored effect of identical furniture.

Half the roll remaining.

13. Alice's torn piece of paper, dropped
to the floor of their childhood room,

covered by an impossibly wide shadow
of Grace and Alice standing together,
or something standing behind them.

Grace remembered not liking the empty hall at their backs as they looked blindly upon their younger selves, both she and her sister turning, arm-in-arm, the door to their room slamming shut behind them with a wall of wind. She'd reached behind her back and had felt the door, wondering if her sister had closed it.

14. An accidental shot of the floor, nearly black, completely covered in shadow despite the camera flash.

"Both Mom and Dad were asleep in bed, right?" Alice asked, and Grace had been thinking the same question because of the next three images, which panned from left to right.

15. The living room, left, with a flat screen television mounted on the wall, powered on and displaying a rerun episode of *The Twilight Zone*, a black-and-white scene with a woman in a train station looking confusedly at her luggage next to a bench.

16. The living room, centered, with a coffee table enveloped by a wraparound couch. A half-empty glass and a remote on the table. An unrecognizable male figure sitting on the couch, hands on his knees, his entire body out of focus, but face turned toward the camera—a completely featureless blur—as if he'd noticed the two of them taking pictures in the dark and had posed with an empty face.

17. The living room, right, with the left-most portion streaked black with heavy contrast covering what should be the couch and the man sitting there, an uncle or family friend staying the night perhaps, the right-most portion revealing the front entryway.

"Who the *hell* is that," Alice said, pointing at the middle picture.

"Maybe Uncle Thomas? He sometimes—"

The next four photographs were unremarkable, despite the fact that they'd captured the memories from sixty years ago. The contrast of each image darkened from one to the next, as if they were progressively underexposed, the last of which was nearly black.

18. The front entryway.

19. The kitchen from far away.

20. A close-up of the left side of the kitchen.

21. A close-up of the right side of the kitchen.

Grace remembered the cold breeze that had once again spun them around, their arms becoming untangled for a few seconds. She'd flailed around in the dark for her sister, and had imagined Alice doing the same. *What happens if I lose her before shifting back?* she'd wondered, and then she'd found her, and had turned the camera around for a selfie from as far out as she could reach.

22. Grace standing next to an older man or older woman, a featureless flowing witch of an apparition, face and hair as black as pitch and eyes glowing inverted white.

"What do you remember?" Grace asked, pulling away from her.

"I remember … losing you but quickly finding you, and I was led to what felt like the front entryway of the house. I remember that because the door opened and it was cold. So cold. And then I was led to the porch and then a *barn*, and the door slammed shut behind us and I remember saying *I don't want to do this!* but you couldn't hear me so I pulled off my blindfold and the headphones and then we were back or coming back and I said, *Don't ever make me do that again.* And we *were* back. Who is that with you in the picture?"

> 23. An accidental shot of their feet after they'd tripped over something while moving through the house—of *Grace's* feet, as there were no other feet but her own.

She and Alice had hastily made their way back to where they'd started by this point. The final photo would be of their parents' bedroom.

But Alice wasn't with me, Grace realized. *I'd imagined her chanting* let's go back let's go back please let's go back, *but it wasn't her, it wasn't Alice who'd led her back so hastily.*

She hesitated with the final picture, too afraid to see, hands shaking.

They'd shifted back. Grace could take physical things with her to the past, and whenever she shifted back, the items would still be with her, as if they'd never left the present. Which meant she didn't necessarily need to *touch* those things to bring them back.

"I came back," Alice said, as if reading her thoughts. "Let's see it. The last picture."

Grace closed her eyes, holding the photo to her chest, took a deep breath, and then she opened her eyes and held it out so they could see it together.

> 24. Their father's side of the bed in the early hours of the morning, his covers thrown to the side, an impression of his head sunken into the pillow. Mom's hand in the frame, reaching out but not finding him, leaning over to where he should be, her eyes open, startled awake. The rest of the bed out of focus, dark clouds of black around the edges, as if from underexposure.

"Where's Dad?" Alice asked, and then, "Did Dad ever, you know—?"

"He must have gotten up, while we were there."

"Did he ever—?"

There were so many questions, yet suddenly not enough time for Alice to ask them all, let alone finish a single thought. Grace understood what her sister wanted to ask, because Grace already *knew*. If Dad had ever taken her from bed at night after everyone else had gone to sleep. If they'd ever go places. If he'd ever touched her. Grace knew what Alice wanted to ask, because she'd asked those same questions after revisiting her childhood.

Grace flipped through the photobook of her father for the first time, watching him age in reverse from old man to young man, sixty years passing in a matter of seconds. She loved him then as she loved him now. She looked from the photobook to the first picture now hanging in the darkroom: Dad at thirty-four; at thirty-four she'd loved him most.

It wasn't until the year 2007 that she'd suspected her father of anything. She'd been thirteen, Alice only twelve, and so she spent a great deal of time shifting back to that year to help her re-remember what she'd forgotten about her youth. And each time she revisited, the past became *darker*, became filled with black tendril shapes and impossible shadows and horrific sounds, as if her past were trying to mask what had happened all those years ago. 2007 is when Grace noticed her father starting to *change*. There was a drastic difference in the way he looked—*or perhaps the way she saw him*—compared to any year after that, so she spent more time in 2007, and then 2006, and then 2005, focusing most on those three years. In the beginning of 2007 he'd become incredibly sad, a part of him missing, and so she'd started there, spending more time with him in that year before going back further into the past.

"Go through the photos," Grace told her sister.

"Start with 2005 and work your way up to the present. I want you to remember Dad one year at a time, and when you feel you understand who he is, who you remember him to be, then we'll both revisit 2004 and take more photos, again, and again, and then we'll go to 2003, and then 2002, as far back as we can go."

"I don't know if I can do this," she said.

"You need to."

Alice picked up the box labeled 2005, which had perhaps four hundred photographs Grace had taken, and developed, just the other day. She sorted through them.

"Look for the ones of Dad."

In 2005 her father sometimes got up in the middle of the night, watched over them while they slept, sometimes standing in the doorway, sometimes sitting at the edge of their bed, brushing either her or Alice's hair, and sometimes he'd simply stand at the window looking out into the dark. These were the photos she wanted her sister to see. These were the photos that would help her understand.

And it would keep her busy for a while.

Grace looked to the new photos of 2004 hanging before her, stared at #16, the faceless blur of a man sitting at the couch. She knew who he was now. She remembered everything.

She closed her eyes, *shifted*.

Without the gauze coverings, without the bandana, without the noise-cancelling headphones, Grace shifted back to that same night in 2004. She wanted to see everything this time, hear everything, because she was no longer afraid.

She knew who her father was and what he had done.

When she opened her eyes again, she was standing next to her parents' bed, looking over her father while he slept. She and her sister had visited this same exact spot, this same exact moment of *time*, and she couldn't help but wonder if she'd maybe see another version of the two of them shift into this plane of existence, but Grace was alone this time, her eyes open, her ears listening.

A melee of swirling black filled the room around her, pumping out like smoke from beneath the bed, reaching out for her impossible presence from every dark crevice like wiry wisps of hair. From every void came the distant screams of children from other wheres and other whens, the nighttime house-settling noises of a hundred versions of the same house overlaid one on top of the other. But Grace wasn't afraid, not this time.

Her father struggled restless under the covers, her mother's hand reaching for him. He yawned and put a hand to his mouth to catch it, opened his eyes. This was the moment she and her sister had taken the second photo, she knew, the one that looked like the painting of *The Scream*. She left him there and followed the blackness, which shifted out of the room like fog and down the hall, as if wanting her to follow.

She found herself admiring the multi-photo picture frames on either side of the hallway, the same older photos she'd taken with newer photos, and she touched the glass of some, as if doing so would bring back those memories even more.

Down the hall she stopped at the bathroom, hesitating before looking to the mirror she knew would be waiting for her. She expected a reflection of her older self, or the reflection of something else entirely standing next to her, but after collecting enough courage to look, she discovered she didn't cast a reflection at all, perhaps because she really wasn't there. Yet there was *something* casting a reflection, another memory perhaps, or a memory of a memory.

If I had the camera with me, she thought. *I'd be able to capture my reflection*, and then the thought was gone, for the layer upon layer of screaming intensified down the hall. The darkness deepened behind her, passed through the hall and toward the bedroom door with the KEEP OUT sign—like a warning.

The door was ajar, and so Grace again hesitated. Some of the black from within the room emerged and brushed against her hand, like the backs of two fingers gently caressing her skin. *Come inside*, the invisible hand gestured. *Come inside.*

Grace pushed the door inward and found her childhood bedroom engulfed in the smoky cloud-like substance, some of which had escaped through the door as soon as she'd opened it, and some of which moved from one side of the room to the other—from Alice's side of the tape to her own side. The window ahead, like the bathroom mirror, did not cast Grace's older shadow, but something was *there*. Outside the wind howled, and this startled her little sister awake; nine-year-old Alice sat upright, a nearly perfect ninety-degree angle, and looked sleepily around the room, toward Grace's bed. She said "*Grace?*" but the older sister Alice wanted wasn't there, although her older self *was* and wanted to answer. *I'm here, Alice*, she thought, *I'm here*, but younger Grace was gone, her bed a tangle of disturbed blankets. Alice rubbed her eyes and yawned her own little scream.

A shriek cut through the sudden silence, and as Grace turned to the noise behind her, she saw terror in Alice's face as she raced out of bed and slammed the door, as loud as a gunshot.

Grace made her way to the living room because that's where the darkness took her, twisting and coiling like a snake, to the television playing an episode of *The Twilight Zone*—only on, she discovered, to mask the noise, to help cover what was happening—and to the couch, where the black shapeless form she'd been following transformed into the silhouette of a man, their Uncle Thomas, whose head turned toward her, his face solid for a moment and then featureless, then dissolving and moving toward the front entryway of the house with another smaller shape at his side, holding a smoke-billowing hand, a little girl screaming *I don't want to do this! I don't want to do this!* even over the cacophony of noises, even over the layers upon layers of painful memories from the cold winters of 2004, and the years leading up until then.

I don't want to do this!

Grace followed the black apparition, followed the *scream*, found herself following the phantasms of Uncle Thomas and the dragged girl through the door and out onto the front porch.

I was led to what felt like the front entryway of the house. I remember that because the door opened and it was cold. So cold. And then I was led to the porch and then a barn and the door slammed—

Grace followed them into the vacant barn next door. She and Alice used to play there as children, even though they weren't supposed to. They hadn't had neighbors for as long as she could remember, the neighbor's house dilapidated, their barn in decent shape. She and Alice used to play in the barn and pile the abandoned hay as high as they could manage, sometimes ten feet tall and ten feet around, and they'd climb the rickety wooden stairs to the loft and jump and fall and laugh until they were tired and cold.

So cold.

And this is where he dragged the arm of the little girl, deeper into the barn—illuminated only by flashlight—and behind the tractor, and this is where Grace followed them, and *heard*, and *saw*—a black swirling melee of painful memories finally taking shape, Uncle Thomas, not her father … and a little girl, and not Alice, but ten-year-old Grace, her younger self.

How long had this been happening?

The older version of Grace turned around and met the eyes of her father, the version of him she'd always wanted to remember, the version she loved most, his light beaming onto her like an oncoming train. Perhaps Alice slamming the bedroom door had stirred him out of sleep, had caused him to check in on the girls like he always had, only to find *one* of his girls sleeping, not two, only to find his brother no longer on the living room couch although the television was still on, perhaps looking outside because the front door was ajar, and perhaps he'd seen the flashlight beam, heard his oldest daughter's scream …

Her father carried a wrench, the red heavy kind used for large pipes. He walked right through the seventy-year-old version of Grace and for a split second she felt both his understanding and his anger—could feel his rage developing—and she watched as he brought the wrench over his head and swung downward, and then suddenly the chaos of noise ceased.

"Come on, sweetie," he said. "Let's get you dressed and inside."

It wasn't until this memory that Grace realized she'd been involved.

She'd only thought Alice.

Go through the photos, Grace told her sister before shifting to this memory. *Start with 2005 and work your way up to the present. I want you to remember Dad one year at a time, and when you feel you understand who he is, who you remember him to be …*

Grace wanted Alice to figure out that she—*not Grace*—had been molested by their uncle. She'd first photographed the act in the summer of 2007, and through the developed film had determined he'd been doing it from as early as the winter of 2004— the when and where they'd shifted to together—a span of nearly three years. Alice had never spoken of it, *ever*, as if the events had never happened, as if she didn't *know* what had happened to her all those years ago, which is why Grace had invited Alice along this time. She needed her sister to remember. If Alice looked through the pictures of her father, she'd stumble on their uncle and—

"Let's get you inside," her father repeated.

She watched her father—half her own age—

remove his jacket and wrap it around the small arms of her shivering ten-year-old self, watched them walk back to the house. And then she found herself looking over her uncle, unconscious next to the tractor, next to the haystacks where she and Alice used to play. All those smiles. All those laughs. All those *good* memories. He was bleeding, but not enough. Grace wanted the wrench, to smash it against his head, again and again and again … but she wasn't really there. She stood over him for what seemed an impossible amount of time, willing him to bleed out, willing him to die.

And then her father was suddenly there again, eyes red and face wet, standing next to Grace with a hand on his hip and the other pressing against his temples, standing close enough that she could feel radiance pouring out of him, his love. "God*dammit*, Tom," he said, and that was it, as if cursing his brother's name and not his god. He leaned his weight onto his other foot. Looked to the wrench. Contemplated. Hesitated. He retrieved the wrench and it was heavy enough to warrant resting against his shoulder. Her father sniffed back the tears and grabbed the handle with both hands, knuckles whitening. He cried, lifted the heavy thing over his head, cried some more. He made as if to swing it over his head, but simply let it drop and fell to his knees. Uncle Thomas began to stir then, and groan, and once again her father looked to the wrench.

Kill him, Grace thought, *kill the bastard*, but she knew he wouldn't.

When her uncle came to, her father lifted his brother onto his feet and waited for him to realize the gravity of the situation, to realize he *knew*, and once that happened, signified by the startled expression on her uncle's face, her father grabbed him by the collar and punched him in the jaw, in the face, again and again and again, keeping him upright to take the blows—Uncle Thomas' mouth drooling scarlet, eyes vacant—and then he let him crumple to the ground. "I should *kill* you," he said, but didn't, and never would.

She knew because Grace had seen her uncle in future years. Sometime after this near-death beating, he'd gone through *the system* to overcome *his problem* and Mom and Dad—*never Dad and Mom*—for some reason had let the monster back into their lives, because he was *family*, even letting him live in their garage for a period of time. And Uncle Thomas would not recover, but would repeatedly molest her little sister over the next few years, enough so that Alice to this day could not remember, or had somehow blocked it from her memory.

How can you not remember something so bad? she wondered, hating her sister for it. *How many times does it take before you tune it out, before you completely forget?*

And now Grace hated her*self*, wondering *How*

many times did it happen to me, and how can I not remember something so bad?

Grace wouldn't stop until she knew the answers; she'd go back, and back, and back, without the blindfolds, without the ear protection; she wasn't scared of the dark; she'd see and hear *everything* from now on. And she'd try to get her sister to do the same.

Should have killed him, Dad, Grace thought, shifting back to the darkroom.

"You went back," Alice said.

"I did."

"And you *saw*, and *heard*," she said, pointing at the items on the table.

Alice stood over the box marked 2007. Next to it were boxes for 2006 and 2005. She'd gone through the last three years' worth of photography, and by the look in her eyes, she *knew*.

"I did," Grace said, "and it happened to *me*, too."

She added the latest picture of their father to the back of the flipbook, and slowly passed through the last sixty years of his life, watched him turn from the ninety-four-year-old she'd watched die last spring to the thirty-four-year-old from her latest shift to the past. She watched him change, watched the sadness and the pain take over his features in the earlier years. Flipping from back to front, he aged as she'd watched him do in life.

Grace set down the book and looked at her

sister. No words needed to be spoken, there was just a shared understanding of the situation. She grabbed the bandana and the gauze she'd worn these last sixty days, threw them in the trash, and then hugged her sister.

"We need to go back," Alice said.

"We need to know when all of this started."

"And we need to know when it stopped."

"You're really going with me," Grace said, not as a question, and then she led her little sister upstairs and into the light.

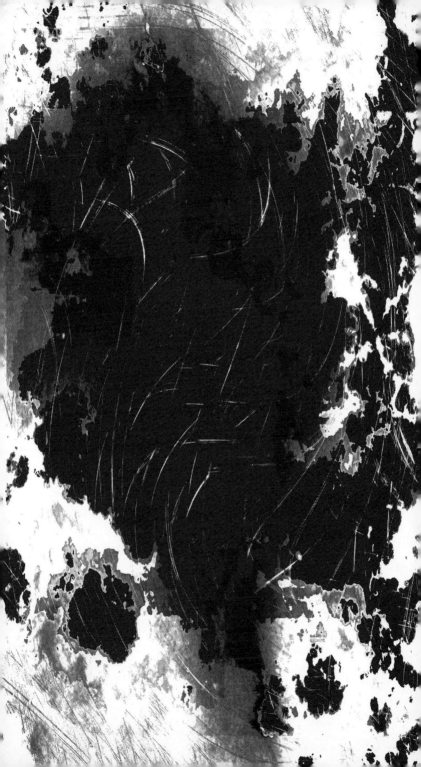

SAD FACE

Yuliya dons the plastic face. Scents of the oil-blend lining the interior—lavender, bergamot, vetiver, chamomile, rose, and frankincense—work symbiotically with the prosthetic, the mask not only disguising her expression but the wet city stench as it soothes. She breathes heavily, systematically, through a slit behind a set of false lips. She holds the fake plastic face against her real face, not worrying about the straps this time, simply pressing the rubbery texture hard against her nose and mouth, like an oxygen mask. She counts three seconds of inward breath—

(three blocks from the car, three, the magical number)

—and counts three more as she breathes out, her fingers shaky. And then another three-second inward breath and Yuliya remembers the effects of the oils as explained to her from a close friend, Ylang, an addict of alternative medicines. *One*: the lavender, how it calms tension, and can work wonders on the nervous system; *two*: the bergamot, how it induces relaxation, reverses agitation—something about *corticosterone*, but she can't quite remember because her friend is a loon—as she takes in the floral aromas; and *three*: vetiver, whatever the hell *that* may be, how it can ground you with its energy, yet decrease hypersensitivity and jitteriness. She holds the air in her lungs for another three seconds—

(the car, will it start, of course it will start, and the keys, yes, in the purse, she discovers rifling through, not misplaced, not lost, not—oh god, who's that?—she wonders)

—and counts three more as she breathes out, remembering the essentials. *One*: chamomile, a peaceful scent, how it eases anxiety and worrisome thoughts; *two*, rose, how its oil does some sort of mystical shit; *three*, frankincense, how it can bring the mind tranquility and spiritual grounding or something, a "quieter of the mind," Ylang claimed.

She takes a wide berth to avoid the couple walking toward her. They pass by, both turning their heads to stare, perhaps wondering about the nervous woman holding not her *real* face, but her *SAD* face.

Yuliya had dug the prosthetic from her purse, frantically covering the face she didn't want the world to see with a face the world had seen a year ago. They'd taken a mold and created a skin of her year-ago face to adhere to the top of this one—a digital image printed like a sticker, the type of material one would use to personalize a cellphone or laptop. She could've had other faces printed, other *skins*, but the first was considered covered care and any additional skins were under elective coverage and would cost money she didn't have for each new face.

So she had only one *SAD* mask, what she always thought of as her *SAD* face: a Yuliya Pakinov mask, designed to assist with social anxiety disorder, hence the name.

The fake face was a snapshot of her past. Time, it can only stop when someone takes a photo, and that's what they did, whoever made it—took her picture and made her a mask to hide behind whenever social phobia bullied her. She thought of it as her *dead-face*: expressionless, her eyes visible through open sockets, the mouth slightly parted. The way she imagined she'd look the day she died. And now, whenever someone sees her—*stares* at her—wearing her Yuliya mask, they are looking at her past—

(always looking, evaluating, judging)

"What!" she yells at the couple, not a question,

but an accusation, and now *they* are the ones taking the wide berth, stepping into the street, in fact, into the puddles.

Behind her *SAD* face, she sometimes finds confidence.

Yuliya breathes in and out, audibly, through slits in the plastic.

Breathe through your mouth at first, focus on counting. Your chest, it will rise and fall for as long as your mind is conscious of your body breathing, of simply thinking about the air passing through your lungs …

Along with the sound of her breath against the mask, Yuliya hears her heartbeat, feels it pounding at her eardrums, looks down and notices her chest rising and falling, and she can't stop thinking about it, about breathing, can't stop focusing on the fact that she's looking at herself, and thinking about herself, about things that should come naturally, and this over-self-analyzing, this over-self-realizing—

Tell someone not to think about breathing and they will do the opposite; they will concentrate on breathing, like you are doing now, mechanically exaggerating what normally occurs automatically, unconsciously, without thought …

The repetition of keywords in her last session with Ylang were intentional, Yuliya realizes as she tries to fall back into her mediation. The redundancy of phrase, the softly-spoken choice of words, each gently drawn-out near-whisper, both therapeutic and hypnotizing—

Close your mouth, breathe through your nose instead …

Closing her mouth allows the oil-blend lining the mask to refocus her thoughts. She breathes through two noses this time while taking in the various scents.

Focus on a single object, or close your eyes and find a focal point within that darkness …

Closing her eyes, she wonders if the man at her car can see that her eyelids are painted to look like her eyes are open. Even without the mask, each time she blinks—a third of a second—her eyes appear open, always watching.

Eventually, the mind wanders and awareness is lost, and breathing will once again occur naturally, only your stomach will rise and fall, you will breathe out your nose, allowing you to take in the …

Lavender, rose, bergamot.

Now open your eyes …

The couple is long gone by now, well behind her, but she can feel them like the cold, staring over their shoulders, and she can imagine their whispered conversation:

"Did you see her face?"

"She was wearing something over it."

"Covering her face."

"A mask."

"I wonder if she's burnt or scarred under there."

She sees her car, the clunker Honda Civic with peeling sunburnt bronze paint, and it too stares at

65

her, but with complexity: one headlight lower than the other, the front bumper split like a cleft lip, the entire vehicle sagging toward the driver's side from a past accident.

A man stands next to her wreck of a car, and this stops her a block away. The crosswalk sign illuminates a white walking man to let her know it's safe to cross—as safe as any street in the city can be to cross—but she stays at the curb, looking over her shoulder and around to make sure she stands alone. He's simply standing there, rocking on the balls of his feet, as if waiting for her. Some kind of vaping device dangles from his mouth, which he holds like a joint and

(she inhales heavily)

the tip glows blue for a moment before

(she exhales heavily)

expelling a white cloud that evaporates into the night. He looks into the passenger window, adjusting his hair against the reflection perhaps, or is he peering in and looking at the file box on the front seat, wondering what's inside, only pretending to fix his hair?

Try not to think about the man at your car who wants to kill you and the opposite will happen ...

The crosswalk sign transforms from a man—the image of a walking woman would be too expensive, more LEDs required to make the dress and all—to a hand, blinking at the very edge of her periphery with its orange number countdown, like a heart-beat, because she can't help but focus on the man at her car:

[blink] : 10

/ *What's he doing and what did I leave for him to find what does he want there's nothing on the front seat other than the*

[blink] : 09

/ *box from work packed to overflowing with personal belongings after the exit interview with both human resources and her direct supervisor*

[blink] : 08

/ and the man by the car lit by a lonely streetlamp turns to her for the briefest of seconds and looks her in the eyes from a block away before her mind wanders

[blink] : 07

/ *"We want to emphasize this has nothing to do with your medical cond—"* because such things would be highly illegal to fire someone over

[blink] : 06

/ *"We don't feel the mask is appropriate work attire as outlined in the employee handbook you signed when you were hired"* and the entire experience seems just as fragmented now as it was then like a personal attack over something as stupid as

[blink] : 05

/ *"Section 3.4.12 covers unnatural color hair-dying, visible tattoos, body piercings, gauges, or any other such perceptible body modifications, and under clothing quote* 'hats and other such objects covering the head and / or face' *unquote"* like a panic attack

[blink] : 04

/ they attacked her and she panicked, said things no one would ever considering—

[blink] : 03

/ *"This is who I am!"* and *"Fuck off!"* and other screaming on her end and calm peaceful soft-speak from their end

[blink] : 02

/ *"You've been written-up for this behavior in the past on three separate accounts. The first offense went unrecorded after you agreed not to wear the mask at your workspace because it was frightening some of your peers. The fact that you're wearing the mask during this—"*

[blink] : 01

/ And then silence as the mask did what it's designed to do: to *mask* her feelings and her emotions and her tears, to give her confidence.

[blink] : 00

The blinking orange hand turns solid and the numbers cease flashing. And the man by her car tucks the fake cigarette into his shirt pocket, starts to walk away, as if parapsychologically, or perhaps telepathically, sensing her every thought.

What had she put in the box?

What personal belongings had she taken?

Yuliya had always been careful at work: diligently covering the Celtic knot tattoo on her ankle with an oversized Band-Aid whenever wearing anything other than long pants, a smaller bandage covering the semicolon tattoo on her wrist, and making sure the hesitation marks on both arms were always hidden behind long sleeves—despite summer temperatures, despite her cubicle at the westernmost side of the building, the one with the inoperable window where they'd placed her, the sun always beating against her and creating a parallelogram glare on her monitor.

She remembered folding together the file box she'd gotten from the supply closet, the walk back to her cubicle and the way everyone whispered to each other and glowered as she passed. She remembered placing the file box on her desk and tossing things into it: a stapler—which they'd taken back at the exit door because it featured a company label, a picture frame with the original stock photo because she hadn't filled it, a black plastic weight that held paper upright so she could transcribe—which they tried taking at the door but let her keep, a stack of personal papers—which they'd thumbed through, a black mug with TODAY IS YESTERDAY'S TOMORROW printed on one side and TODAY IS TOMORROW'S YESTERDAY printed on the other in white lettering, various pens she'd collected over the years, an inspirational desk calendar, and other junk. Had she taken anything else?

She doesn't remember putting anything else in the box, and of course that gets her mind thinking about what else she may have put in the box.

Try not to think about giraffes fucking and the opposite will happen …

DO NOT WALK the crosswalk sign reads under a bright orange hand, like a premonition.

You'll have trouble getting it out of your head.

The man walking away from her car turns around once again, facing her, hesitating, like the marks on her wrist. He looks directly at her with a look that says, "You'd never approach me anyway so I'll just smash-and-grab" and leans against the car.

A giraffe awkwardly mounting another.

He takes something from his pocket, something that barely fits in his hand, something silver with a point, looks around once more, and smashes out her passenger side window with a *pop*. The car's old but has safety glass, which spider-webs and tinkles to the ground, most of it going into the front seat.

WALK the crosswalk sign reads again under the familiar illuminated man, *daring* her, but she stays at the curb. She breathes in through her nose and it's loud, the scent of vetiver filling her nostrils and working its way to the back of her throat. The vetiver offers energy, courage … enough to step onto the street. Whatever vetiver *is*, it tastes awful.

She's midway across the intersection when the man leans in through the Civic's broken passenger window, rifling through her stuff, his body half in and half out the vehicle. Something white falls from his front pants pocket, dislodged from leaning against the sill, but he's too distracted to notice. Whatever it is, he steps on it a few times, and then pulls the entire box out of the car and doesn't notice Yuliya walking toward him, but the thought of this man noticing her stops her in place, in the middle of the road. She looks through the mask to the ground, afraid to look up and meet his eyes. Perhaps if she stays perfectly still he won't notice. Enough time's passed that the sign blinks the last of another countdown, the metal box buzzing like power lines each time the numbers appear:

[blink] : 03

/ "Stop!" cuts off in her throat and it sounds like the beginning of a stutter, not even loud enough to carry the half-block remaining between them and

[blink] : 02

/ he hurries to his own car parked a few spaces behind her Honda, a silver crossover of some kind hiding just outside a triangle of shine offered by the streetlight, and the hatchback opens remotely from his key fob while she's

[blink] : 01

/ holding her breath …
/ holding her breath …
/ holding her breath …

[blink] : 00

Headlights approach from the street she's not yet crossed and she's still looking at the ground, focusing on the smallest of puddles—shaped like a cigarette burn, like the one on her thigh, the one she'd put there to cope for the crowd of—

Focus on a single object or close your eyes and find a focal point somewhere within that darkness …

She keeps her eyes open, on that spot.

A bumper comes to a stop a few inches from slamming into her knee and there's a soft squeal of brakes and her hand goes out instinctively in a gesticulation mocking the orange DO NOT WALK hand glowing just outside her periphery. She doesn't really *see* the car until it honks for her to get out of the way. Yuliya quick-steps to the curb and waves an apology to the car—not the person behind the wheel—that almost hit her, finally remembering to breathe.

Your chest, it will rise and fall for as long as your mind is conscious of your body breathing, of simply thinking *about the air passing through your lungs …*

She realizes the honk is loud enough to carry the half-block remaining between her and the man at her car and she closes her eyes to make him go away. Tightly she closes her eyes, her chest rising and falling because she can't help but concentrate on her breathing, on the realization that her chest is rising and falling. He's staring at her now, she knows. Her eyes are closed, but don't look closed thanks to the mask. Does he recognize her? *(a car door opens)*. Does he drop the box? *(a car door slams shut)*. Does he sense her fear? *(an engine erupts to life)*. Does he flee? *(speeds off)*. The panic forms her hands into fists, her lungs to deflate, every single one of her joints to buckle *(tires squealing far away, in some parallel universe)*. A half-dozen questions / concerns rush in at once: Is he walking toward me or away does he have a gun a knife a screwdriver can you see my eyes my eyes are closed go away go away why my box my personal possessions the pens and mug and stapler—not the stapler they took the stapler—and picture frame displaying stock-photo strangers I have no friends no friends no one to understand my cond—s*hut up shut up shut up SHUT UP!—go away please go away whoever you are you're fine you're fine, now open your eyes, close your fake eyes and open your real eyes.*

Her fake eyes flutter closed so her real ones can flutter open.

He's gone.

Yuliya stands under the crosswalk sign buzzing its latest countdown; the backs of her shaky hands—she holds them out—reflect fake-tan orange with every blink. She breathes out ... breathes in ... breathes out ... breathes in ... deep and heavy and concentrated upon until her skin glows solid fake-tan orange. She imagines the illuminated hand somewhere above, signaling her to stop: DO NOT PANIC. And when the orange glow turns white, she imagines the illuminated walking man is there to let her know it's safe to WALK again—as safe as any sidewalk in the city can be to walk. And so she walks, her flats slapping wet concrete.

Little cubes of blue-green glass litter the gutter. The majority of the mess had made it into the car, sprinkled like confetti on the seats, the floor and cup holders—as if the window had exploded and not simply *popped*; some even made it onto the dash and backseats. The file box was gone, and everything she'd taken from her cubicle at work. He'd taken everything.

It's gone it's all gone all of it but are the things in that box important what was in there really just a bunch of junk collected over the years and who cares about that shit it's just shit it's nothing it's nothing the picture frame was something a gift from someone (at work?) but the people in the photograph were nothing but model-perfect fake plastic people probably dead and gone and divorced or at least unhappy.

Nothing in the box mattered.

Who'd take such garb—

But he'd left something behind: what had fallen from his pocket as he'd jimmied himself inside. In the gutter, amidst the crushed-ice-cube-like glass of her Civic waits a pocket-crumpled note written in oversized childish blocky letters, handwriting she quickly recognizes because the size of the lettering is uneven, and then she quickly recognizes what's written:

STARBUCKS ON H AND 14TH
CRAPPY HONDA CIVIC, GOLD (?)
1LVJ196

The streets are empty and Yuliya stands vulnerably under the triangle of light offered by the streetlamp. *Come and get me!* the spotlight says. The signal lights continue to change from green to yellow to red and repeat, despite a lack of traffic, their light haze reflecting off the asphalt. This is how she enjoys the world: empty.

Frankincense, she thinks, taking in the scent, before removing the mask and tossing it through the open—*there is no*—window. Her hands are still shaky, but with rage.

She reads the note / instructions again and tosses that, too, into her CRAPPY HONDA CIVIC, GOLD (?). She can never remember her license plate by heart, but the letters and numbers match her front plate as she walks around to the driver's side door.

Julia Moran.

They'd met once for coffee at the Starbucks on H and 14th, but by accident. Yuliya was a creature of habit, every Friday night after work donning the *SAD* mask and following Ylang's advice by forcing herself into society, which she did weekly, religiously, for nearly a year, including tonight. She'd order a hot decaf tea—extra-hot, Tazo or something, never coffee because of the jitters; not a good thing to have while fighting anxiety—and she'd look for one of the corner-facing tables, move the second chair to another table so no one could sit next to her, and she'd take in the chaotic noises of society, including the two-dozen or so simultaneous conversations that came with it. There she'd sit, for an hour or so, waiting for the tea to cool enough to sip, and she'd sip until it was gone. She'd hide behind her *SAD* face, sometimes with her eyes closed, sometimes not, depending on the noise. No one ever questioned her about the mask, although sometimes she'd get fingers pointing her way from kids whose parents would then lead them away, and eventually she became a regular—the sad girl in the corner with social issues, the freak behind the mask. And then she'd go home, to where it was safe.

Yuliya Pakimov?

She'd collided with Julia Moran as she'd turned with her tea after paying for it, nearly spilling 210° Tazo-berry-something all over her, and her heart had stopped … well, felt as though it had stopped. It was the first time anyone from work had ever seen Yuliya wearing her *SAD* face. She'd only started wearing it to work in recent months.

Is that you?

Julia worked—had—in the cubicle next to hers.

It is *you. What are you doing here? You're getting something to drink, well duh! What—what is that, the mask?*

Is that one of those … self-efficacy things?

Pfizer had created a memorable commercial.

One good thing about extroverts is that they do all the talking around introverts.

She'd tried leading Yuliya to a table in the center of the room, but Yuliya pulled away and found a table in the far corner opposite the restrooms. She'd quickly learned the table closest to the restrooms, while it seemed the most secluded, came with wafting smells and long lines of people who couldn't help but do their best to look-but-not-look at her as they waited their turn. Julia had tried her best not to stare at the mask that night, but, like the rest, she couldn't help herself, and was intrigued.

They made it look just *like you. It's so*
(freaky)
different, and … you. I didn't even know you had
(issues)
a difficult time with social settings. You don't wear it at work, so …

She'd left it hanging, perhaps hoping for some returned conversation. Everything Julia'd said came out politically correct, almost passable for sincere, but Yuliya understood how PC was simply an acronym for 'fucking ridiculous,' and how pauses between words, and inflection, unmasked truth.

She'd rather hear truth than listen to someone dance around it.

Mind if I sit with you?

She had minded, but nodded anyway because she needed conditioning, after all. If she ever wanted to get better, if that were even remotely possible, she'd dance the dance.

I can't believe how real it looks. I mean, how much like the ...

(real / damaged / broken)

how much it looks like Yuliya Pakimov. I have a friend whose older brother has one. He's some kind of ...

(idiot)

savant. He had an accident when he as twelve and doctors say he has some kind of acquired savant syndrome. He's super smart, but not comfortable around other people. So Jessica's mom—my friend, Jessica—got him a mask, and it looks just like him. He has a bunch of other faces though, so every time I see him he looks different, which I guess is one of the reasons the mask helps. He has trouble looking people in the eye. I guess you probably do, too.

Yuliya does, her eyes often jump around to anything other than another set of eyes. "Look at me, Yuliya," her mother used to say, grabbing her chin enough to hurt. "Look at me when I'm talking to you," she used to say until she'd died. Her father used to say the same thing, until he understood it was a common trait in those with autism, even the slightest of cases.

But that's

(embarrassing)

okay. We have drugs for pain, so why not facemasks to

help with social anxiety? Modern medicine is pretty cool if you think about it.

Julia's single-sided conversation was only one of the dozen conversations Yuliya had heard simultaneously that night, a trait found in those with social anxiety disorders, those with Asperger's, those with all levels of autism: the inability to filter out unwanted noise, the unbridled need to take them all in at once, to hear *every*thing, every conversation, every minute sound, the hiss of steaming milk, the percolation of coffee, the grinding of beans, the register, the sipping of straws, the stirring of sticks, the taps of laptop keyboards, the calling out of drink orders, the inability to not listen to every goddamn sound ever made.

From far away you can

(point and laugh)

barely tell you're wearing it. Up close you can only tell around the eyes. I guess that's why they call them 'skins,' huh, because they basically look just like your skin, only there's not much expression, which I guess is also part the point in wearing them in public, so you don't have to worry about how people might react to your feelings. Can I

(peel the skin)

touch it?

She'd reached out to touch the *SAD* face, but Yuliya had pulled away.

Sorry. I was just curious what it felt—

"No, it's okay," Yuliya had said, the only words

she'd said that night in the Starbucks on H and 14th.
She'd leaned back in her chair, removed the black
elastic straps hiding within her hair, and took off
her fake face, handing it to the rambling young
woman.

Julia had turned it over a few times, inspecting
both sides.

I didn't expect it to be so

(fake)

real, I guess. And form-fitting. And hard.

She'd tapped it a few times with the back of her
finger, a sound like flicking plastic, and then held
the mask in front of Yuliya, at arms-length, and
with one eye closed—Yuliya passing quick glances
at her through the eye sockets—peered through
those same eye sockets from the other side, aligning Yuliya's fake face with her real face.

It's beautiful, really. You are

(ugly)

beautiful.

That had been enough social experimenting for
the night. Without saying anything, Yuliya took
back the *SAD* mask and reaffixed it to her face,
taking special care with the elastic straps, taking
her time while her heart thrummed. Julia remained
quiet for a change, confused at the sudden abrupt-
ness, perhaps. She stood to leave and Julia stood
with her.

You come here every *Friday?*

And that's how Yuliya knew it was her. Julia Moran knew her routine. She was the *only* one who knew besides a few regulars at that particular Starbucks, and whomever Julia told after that night seeing her there, after touching her *SAD* face. The man at her car, the asshole who'd broken her window and had stolen her file box of personal belongings gathered after she'd been fired ... Julia had planned all that. She had to've. And the handwriting, those childish uneven block letters—she must have written the note. *But why?*

"I need a new face," she tells Ylang early the next morning.

Emotional psychotherapy is fortunately covered by her medical plan, she's told—alternative medicine included—and it might take some time for her termination paperwork to go through. Lori Bahn, her now previous HR Manager, had mentioned temporary GAP coverage and something about Cobra, but the details of the exit interview are a blur. How long would it take for her insurance company to catch up with her termination?

"Your insurance covers 50% of elective coverage items," she tells Yuliya. "Only the mask and first skin is covered the full amount."

"What if this one breaks?"

"The mask is steel cord reinforced plastic. You

couldn't break your face if you tried. And the *skin* is made from Tyvek and Tyvek's made from woven high-density polyethylene plastic `fiber. Flexible, untearable, water resistant, you name it. DuPont doesn't mess around."

"What about the old face? What if it fades or something?"

"The old face?"

"If the printing gets messed up, or sun-bleached, melted or scratched. What if the printing on the mask gets ruined somehow? You'd think it would be in the best interest of the patient, *me*, for social interaction, for self-expression, for confidence—"

"What are you trying to accomplish, Yuliya?"

"And it would be nice to have a backup face that doesn't look like my own. One of my coworker's nephews has half a dozen, and she says it seems to help him because of the anonymity it provides him in public. It's *hiding*, I know, hiding who I am and what I look like behind the mask, but maybe it will get me to interact with society more regularly if I'm not so reliant on a single *skin*. And it would be comforting to know I had a backup, in case something … happens."

"What do you believe might happen?"

Yuliya ignores the question because the conversation isn't going anywhere. She'll need a prescription refill to get her by if she's cut off by her insurance carrier.

She knows Ylang prefers alternative medicines over drugs, hence the essential oils with which Yuliya lined her *SAD* face, but had tried her on selective serotonin reuptake inhibitors (SSRIs), *paroxetine* and *sertraline*, better known as Paxil and Zoloft, and later found that *venlafaxine*, a serotonin and norepinephrine reuptake inhibitor (SNRI), was more effective to prevent more severe panic attacks. She'd heard and used these words so many times in her daily routine they became part of her vernacular. The latter drug, the Effexor XR, seemed to work best to calm her anxiety mid-attack, whether designed to do that or not; perhaps the simple thought of taking the pills had some sort of nearly-instant placebo-like effect.

"I spilled the Effexor last night, in the street after the break-in with my car. My hands, they shook so hard the bottle fell after fucking with the cap and they spilled in the street. I took one anyway, and it helped, but the others, they dissolved like aspirin because the street was wet from the rain … I'll need

(to lie)

a refill." From her purse she pulls the empty orange prescription bottle; she'd emptied the pills into a plastic bag earlier that morning.

After a hesitation, Ylang says, "You're probably low on your beta blockers as well. I want to try a different dosage to see how it works against the epineph—your *adrenaline*."

"And *benzodiazephine?*"

Their eyes meet, but for only a moment before Yuliya looks away, fingers fiddling with the mask in front of her.

"I'm not even sure how you know that word, since I haven't prescribed that to you in the past, if ever in my profession, but no, I want to stay away from *benzodiazephines* for the time being. They work quickly, as you've probably read online, but they are quickly habit-forming. I'm not going to turn you into a junkie. And they'd prohibit you from driving because they are essentially sedatives."

Ylang pulls out her prescription pad—preferring to handwrite scripts the old-fashioned way—and scribbles the long words in legible loopy cursive.

"As for your face, your *mask*, I mean … you can try contacting your carrier directly, maybe shoot your doctor a message. See what they can do."

> *Ms. Pakimov,*
> *We regret to inform you that your request for an additional printing has been denied for the following reason(s): Patient is not currently a member of Kaiser Perman—*

"Call her," she says through the mask. "Dr. Ylang Thiessen. Y-L-A—"

"I'm sorry, but the prescription's not valid," says the man behind the counter, sliding back the script. "The computer is showing that your medical record number has expired. It's a group membership, so you'll need to consult your employ—"

Yuliya dry-swallows one of the pills from the plastic bag.

Sulfuric acid, she thinks, placing the *SAD* face into the glass Pyrex bowl and a white disposable mask over her nose and mouth, like the ones worn by the pharmacy techs at the hospital. The fake face stares up at her—an expressionless Yuliya Pakimov—as if she's looking into a mirror, although her mock reflection's eyeless. H_2SO_4.

A quick Google search on her phone had brought up a list of common acids and where to find them. Sulfuric acid could be found in car batteries, purchased from various auto parts stores, but a stronger, less-diluted form could be purchased at $8.97 per quart bottle at Home Depot, which is where she went after the pharmacy.

The stuff is made by a company called Theochem Laboratories, Inc., for drain maintenance. The label reads: BUSTER. Concentrated Acid Drain Opener. And in a smaller font below that: *Quickly Dissolves Hair, Paper, Food, Rags, Grease and Other Organic Matter. Safe for Septic and Cesspool Systems when used as directed.* THIS IS A VERY STRONG PRODUCT. *Other items are needed for safe use. Read entire label prior to using this product.* The fonts get smaller further down the bottle. And at the very bottom: SOLUTIONS FOR A CLEANER WORLD ™ printed in white text over a red bar. She reads the rest of the bottle, as directed, wears the protective eyewear and gloves. The product is apparently a formulation of 93% virgin sulfuric acid, and has some sort of corrosive inhibitors to protect drain pipes made of metal or PVC / plastics.

Yuliya can't help but think of the materials used in making her mask, and can't think of a reason why this shouldn't work. She's also reminded of the reuptake inhibitors she's swallowing with every pill, and how much her drugs and sulfuric acid have in common.

She peels off the yellow tape with a red CAUTION CAUTION CAUTION spiraling around the top of the bottle, twists off the cap and the protective seal beneath, and hesitates.

There's no going back, she realizes, and pours the acid into the bowl.

The part of her *SAD* face resembling Yuliya Pakimov fizzes and bubbles, the sulfuric acid eating her fake face. The captured emotionless expression from a year ago starts to dissolve, and after ten minutes the murky liquid stills. Reaching in with the protective gloves, she pulls out the mask, and admires the horrific remains. The *skin* part of the mask resembles a fire-melted doll, and peels / rubs away easily enough, like a sunburn.

What lies beneath is a blank, bone-white face-mask.

She cleans off the rest of the curls of acid-eaten fake skin and remembers staring at the white mold they'd created over a year ago; after sanding down the imperfections, the mask looked exactly like the one she now held: smooth, featureless, void of emotion …

Hold very still and take a deep breath, which you'll need to hold for the next few moments. We're going to take a mold of your face. This will take about forty-five seconds.

Her eyes had been closed and covered with protective solid-black goggles that barely fit over each socket, with a small string holding them together, like swimmer goggles, but designed to blackout the room. She'd started holding her breath sooner than needed, her mouth closed while they'd poured what felt like hot wax over her entire face, which burned, burned so bad, but she couldn't cry out as they dabbed at her face with spatulas or wooden sticks of some kind, pressing the scalding malleable material against her skin. She continued holding her breath as it sealed around her nostrils and mouth.

You're doing good, Yuliya. Another thirty seconds or so.

They'd suffocated her—the material rapidly

hardening, adhering, filling every pore—with her every airway obstructed when all she'd wanted was a single breath. She remembered gripping the armrests, digging into them with her fingernails, her elbows and knees wanting to stretch, to move, to not be constrained. She let go of the reclined dentist-like chair, her hands coiling and uncoiling to and from fists, the only thing her body could do to keep from

(dying)

freaking out and it took all her strength not to reach up to her melting face and claw away the lava, and her legs, they wanted to run and to cross and uncross on the footrest and she found herself bending her knees and sliding her feet up the chair and then straddling and planting them on the ground and she wanted to

(die)

run far away but the black world had enveloped her. She'd grabbed the armrests again and un-grabbed them—

Another twenty seconds, you're doing great.

but she wasn't doing great as time slowed while her heart did the opposite. Someone was working an instrument at her nostrils, trying to burrow into them, and another someone was working on her mouth, not panicked like her, but ever so patient, sliding something across her merged lips, their non-rushing hands hidden by her blindness.

Drowning. I'm drowning, she thinks, beating against the chair. Yuliya's hands tried to breathe for her: fist, flat, fist, flat, flashing like a WALK / DO NOT WALK crosswalk sign in her mind, and finally her hands could no longer take it and she brought them up, feeling her face—the material glass-like, hard— and repulsively pulled them back, or perhaps one of the people working over her had pulled them back and—

Another ten seconds, we're almost there.

She'd tried to breathe but the hardening mask wouldn't let her as she counted down the final seconds: *nine, eight, seven,* like Saran wrap wound tightly around her face, *six, five, four,* instruments scraping and scraping and scraping, *three, two, one,* a needle plunging into her nose and a knife slicing apart her lips, and *zero, zero, zero,* she continued to count, thinking *this must be what's it's like for a fish to be pulled out of water,* her internal clock not ticking, but flat-lining—

There we go, someone had finally said, as if that made it better.

And Yuliya had taken in a fast whistling breath through the slit they'd created and tried to reach up again to tear away the suffocating mask, but they'd pulled her arms away, told her it would need to set for a while as they hollowed out a second nostril and widened a temporary mouth. *Couldn't they have put straws in my nose or something in my mouth for air and poured the hot liquid around them*, she'd remembered thinking then. But the mask would have chemically reacted to such materials, her doctor had said, or something similar.

Memories flood through her in this third-person recollection of her past: a young woman's hands returning to their death-grips on the armrests, feet to their crossed positions on the footrest, chest heaving because the woman in the chair couldn't help but think about her own breathing.

Want to see? someone in the dark had said. And feeling high, she'd nodded as that same someone peeled away the blackout goggles, the room exploding in light. A handheld mirror was placed into her hands, which she'd held with both hands.

Hello, old friend.

Sulfuric smells find their way into her sinuses as she's brought back into the now. And that same familiar white mask stares back at her. She'd forgotten to remove the elastic straps from the sides before pouring in the acid; a few remaining strands crumble away.

Her white skinless mold resembles a theatre comedy / tragedy mask, but without the gaping smile / frown, without the captured expression—*her* SAD *face*—and it makes her think of the now-destroyed skin they'd created to place over it—*her dead-face, truly dead.* Gone.

This device will take a three-dimensional rendering of

your face, which will then be used to print a skin *that we'll adhere to the prosthetic. The skins can be easily manu-factured. Simply make an appointment and we can create additional* skins *for your unique prosthetic from donor renderings; depending on your health insurance coverage, they are either relatively inexpensive, or overly expensive.*

She shivers at the thought of *donor* renderings. She'd read something once about the illegality of publically wearing skins from living individuals, and how only donated scans from the deceased could be used on the 'prosthetics'—as her doctor liked calling them, since 'masks' sounded carnival-like— if not donning one's own image.

The blank eyeless face stares up at her, pleading to her to be worn.

After scrubbing the *SAD* face with soap and rinsing it under the bathroom sink faucet, Yuliya dries the white mask with a towel, and places it over her face. She stares at her new self in the mirror, and behind the fake set of colorless lips, she smiles.

Yuliya dons the plastic face. She no longer needs the scents of the oil-blend that once lined the inte-rior—lavender, bergamot, vetiver, chamomile, rose, and frankincense—and now prefers the wet city stench. She breathes calmly, systematically, through the slit in the featureless mouth. She no longer needs to hold the fake plastic face against her real face because the new straps hold it in place just fine. She counts three seconds of inward breath—

(three cars separate them, three, the magical number)

as she follows Julia home after trailing her at the bar, after waiting—parked across the street for nearly an hour—to see the boyfriend or whoever the man was who'd followed Yuliya to the Starbucks on H and 14th, the man who'd broken into her CRAPPY HONDA CIVIC, GOLD (?) to take her box of possessions. Somehow she knew Julia was on her way to see him now, which is why Yuliya had decided to bring the .38 Colt Special she'd taken from her father's gun safe.

What was in the box?

She no longer remembers, no longer cares; she just wants it back

—and counts three more as she breathes out.

Passengers in passing cars stare at her blank face as she follow's Julia's charcoal gray Volkswagen Jetta, but she doesn't mind. *Stare all you want*, her mind tells them. *You're not looking at anyone. A nonentity*, she thinks. *I am no one.*

It's a Friday night and Yuliya realizes Julia's on her way to meet this mystery man for dinner, a date perhaps, based on her texting and the text-reacting smiles while at the bar.

She pulls into the lot of some Italian place called Maggiano's—not a fancy place by any means, but a chain restaurant, a fake fancy place. A fake place for fake people. Julia parallel-parks on the street not far away.

And she waits. And Julia waits.

The sun's already set and the delta breeze rushes cold through the cabin of Yuliya's beat-up Civic. She rolls up the driver's side window—manually rolls because the old thing doesn't have automatic windows—and glances at the broken passenger side window, which isn't broken at all, but whole and *there*. The little green-blue cubes of broken glass are gone as well.

The fuck? she thinks, the gun heavy on her lap.

A silver crossover vehicle, the one from the night before, pulls in behind Julia's Jetta a few car lengths behind and the man inside waves before coming to a complete stop. They both get out, they hug, as if they hadn't seen each other in years.

Yuliya looks down at the Colt, and at the semi-colon on her wrist.

A semicolon is used when an author could've chosen to end their sentence but chose not to. The author is you and the sentence is your life.

She'd read that somewhere, couldn't remember where, but liked the idea. The period portion of her tattoo dotted the area just under the *life line* part of her palm, the comma portion partially covering the end of a white-scar running the length of her forearm. Holding her together, one could say, perhaps connecting her past to her future.

"I'm still alive," Yulia says to the mask in the rearview mirror, hefting the gun.

The disgustingly-cute couple releases their hug and the man leads her to the back, where he lifts open the hatch. Inside is the overflowing brown file box. Julia hugs him again, lifting one leg off the ground at a 90° angle, her toe pointing out. She kisses him on the cheek, and they talk for a bit, Julia sifting through the box, lifting out some papers, the picture frame with the fake people in it, and then putting them back.

Yuliya can tell they're not here for a date; they've only met so he can hand over the box, which Julia moves to the front passenger seat of her

(Jetta)

CRAPPY HONDA CIVIC, GOLD (?). She doesn't bother with the door and simply passes it through the window, which is shatter-broken like her own. The man kisses her on the cheek *goodbye* and Yuliya can feel it on her own like a kiss from the dead, but it's only sweat underneath the mask running down her cheek and she itches it away. Suddenly Yuliya's wrists burn, her joints ache, and she's antsy to get out of the car and move around. The car is claustrophobic and with both windows rolled up—*how can both windows be rolled up?*—her breathing becomes labored and she starts to count the pounding heartbeats.

She closes her eyes, knowing if she could see herself in the mirror, she'd see a blank white face with

(fake)

colorfully-painted eyelids staring back, and when she opens them again, the man and his crossover are gone—*how long had I closed my eyes, only a moment?*

Julia is alone at her car, not a Volkswagen Jetta, but Yuliya's beat-up, sun-blistered gold Honda Civic, highlighted under the triangle of light offered by a lonely streetlight.

I need air, I need air, I need air, her mind drones instead of numbers, and she reaches down to unroll the window a bit, a crack, but there is no handle to grab, only a button to press to bring the window down so she presses the button and the window slides one inch and then two and then three and she counts the gap as it grows, the air thin, stale and wet and nothing like lavender or bergamot or the other oils no longer lining her *SAD* face—*what the hell is happening?*—and like in the chair she balls her hand—the one not holding the gun—into a fist into fist into fist, a little tighter each time, and these fingers, they grip a sweat-soaked wet-crumpled note—*the fuck the fuck the FUCK?*—the size of a marble and slowly, shakily, her fingers uncoil and Yuliya looks down at them. She moves the Colt to the passenger seat without thought, releases a held shuttering breath, and unfolds the wad:

STARBUCKS ON H AND 14TH
CRAPPY HONDA CIVIC, GOLD (?)
1LVJ196

The oversized childish blocky letters are her own, and the license plate matches the one on the crappy Honda Civic. *But*—the steering wheel in front of her now is branded with the letters VW, not an H. Yuliya looks to the crossed street signs at the nearest intersection: one reads 11TH STREET and the other H. In the distance, three blocks away: the green glow of Starbucks.

She pops another pill, thinking of the night at the coffee shop. Julia had peered through the empty eye sockets from the other side of her *SAD* mask, aligning Yuliya's fake face with her real face—*all in my head?* The single-sided conversation in the quiet corner of the coffee shop—*all in my head?*

It's beautiful, really. You are

(ugly)

beautiful.

She had touched her face …

Had she touched her face …

Is that a question or the opposite?

Getting fired, her box of personal belongings, the man breaking into her car, the man no longer here / there, gone in the blink of an eye, and Ylang, the prescriptions, everything …

Is some of it real is most of it real is all of it real?

Yuliya, Julia; the names are even similar.

She watches as Julia gets into her car, looks around, reaches over to the passenger seat, and pulls—*from the box?*—a handgun that looks just like

(Julia's)

her Colt .38 on the passenger seat next to—

The gun is not there, but in Julia's hand, in the other car, and she watches as Julia brings the revolver to the side of her

(*SAD*)

face, hand trembling, finger moving toward—

She can't kill herself no, no, no because if I'm her and she's me and we're somehow tied together she can't no she can't no what does all of this even mean?

Yuliya leans on the horn and it meeps into the night, a week sound, but enough to bring the gun away from Julia's temple and a look of shame—*an emotion, her face has emotion*—and the gun fires but punches a hole through the windshield instead of her head, and she drops the gun. Yuliya's car is the only other around, so of course Julia looks

(at her empty *SAD* face)

her way with tears streaming, and now her own eyes are crying. *But is she seeing me and this white mask of mine / hers / ours or is she seeing herself looking back at me through these black empty eyes?* Yuliya lifts the mask to show her who she is really looking at but before she can reveal herself tires squeal and Julia takes off down the street.

The mask falls back down as Yuliya starts the Jetta to follow.

Julia speeds onto the highway, passing cars erratically, like a game of road slalom, and Yuliya keeps up for the most part, weaving in and out of post-rush-hour traffic. At the last possible moment, the Civic cuts across two lanes and takes EXIT 196A toward the coast. Yuliya misses the exit, but makes EXIT 196B. *Where's she going?* she wonders, and then spots the Civic fishtailing around the street directly in front of her. She's heading toward the ocean. *But where is she going?* she wonders again, and then realizes she already knows. She'd thought of going to the same place before taking the Colt .38 from her father's gun safe.

A brown sign ahead with small white text reads: KEMPER LOOKOUT 2, and for two miles she tries to keep up, the Civic somehow handling the windy corners better than the newer car. Every time Julia's taillights disappear around a bend, Yuliya's headlights fill that void like some kind of light dance of the night. Soon after the KEMPER LOOKOUT 1 sign, she loses her, the taillights no longer illuminating the curves of the road in eerie red. And at the WELCOME TO KEMPER LOOKOUT sign, she realizes why.

The rightmost part of the metal sign is bent back, and the guardrail at the last turn is simply gone. Dust left behind from a ghost car fills the twin beams of her own headlights, which point out to the ocean, out over the lookout.

Yuliya slams on the brakes and skids to a stop in a parking stall, launches out the door and runs to the edge of the fifty-foot drop. It's not a long drop, by any means, but quite a fall for a car launching off the edge. The back of the Civic stares up at her with demon eyes before leveling out, the car a little more than half in and half out of the placid water. The water looks obsidian, the car a mere silhouette cast red in back and white in front, the ocean swallowing the light. The front end of the hood is buckled, but otherwise the car looks like she'd simply parked it in the water. She imagines Julia draped over the steering wheel, forehead bloodied, nose possibly broken, arms pretzeled against the dash. *Air trapped within the cabin keeps the car afloat*, she realizes, *but for how much longer?*

She knows the lookout well, used to go there when she was a kid, and knows about the hiking trail by the wooden marker, It's a quick and easy hike down to the beach below, not visible from the lookout. The lookout simply … *looked out* over the water, and the beach was off to the side quite a bit. She used to race from the bottom of the trailhead to the top with her father whenever leaving for the day, and he'd always let her win—*twenty-seven seconds was her record*—but this late at night she can barely *find* the trail, let alone traverse it. She used to count out the seconds when she was little, and that's what she does now.

Thirty-nine seconds and she's at the bottom, her face protected by the branches and brambles that had pelted her on the descent, her arms scratched all to hell.

The three-quarter moon illuminates the sand as it leads her to the water and she runs toward the car with sand flipping against her back and she's in the Pacific up to her ankles to her shins to her knees and thighs and she dives forward under a wave and waste deep walks out as quickly as the water allows and the next thing she knows she's swimming out, hand over hand, the cold water biting into her. The car, it's starting to tilt

(and will be going down soon)

with the lights flickering and she realizes she's still wearing the *SAD* mask—*although is it still a SAD mask when you acid-burn off the skin?*—as her lungs burn and she reaches out and finds the door handle by pure accident and starts to pull.

Julia's inside, exactly as she'd imagined seeing her, but not unconscious. She leans away from the steering wheel, not yet comprehending what just happened and then all of it sinks in, a look of panic sweeping across her face as her eyes go from the wall of water in front of her to the empty seat and finally to Yuliya, who in turn sees the blank white mask reflected off the driver's side window

because of the moonlight, and through the trans-
parent reflection is Julia, as if she's looking through
the mask from the other side. She tries the door
handle from the inside while Yuliya tries the door
handle from the outside, but the car is in water too
deep for the door to budge.

There's still a lot of air left in the cabin, but not
for long. Seawater races up from the floorboards.
The car tilts more rapidly, nearly nose in / butt out,
as they both work uselessly at the door. Water is up
to her waist and then to her chest. They are both
chest deep in the ocean, Yuliya realizes, when Julia
begins beating on the glass, her mouth an open O
of continuous scream. The last of the lights flicker
out and they are left dark under the moon. Yuliya
pounds hard on the glass from the other side to
get her attention and it takes a while for their eyes
meet. She makes a gun shape out of her hand and
mocks shooting the window. Julia's eyes widen in
understanding and she nods as the car continues
to sink lower. She searches frantically for the gun,
finds it on the passenger floorboard, and holds
it up. The smallest of smiles finds her lips, and
behind the mask, Yuliya mimics her.

Yuliya would have gotten out of the way so she
could have fired the gun, but Julia slams the barrel
over and over again against the glass and on the
third, it shatters, allowing a cascade of water to fill
the shrinking airspace.

Julia's sucked deeper inside and in a single heart-beat disappears.

The car groans as the ocean swallows it whole.

Flipping off the mask, Yuliya dives down, finds the opening and blindly reaches inside, *reaching reaching reaching* and not finding anything. No one is there. She comes up for air, the panic keeping her from taking much breathe, but she takes as much as she can and dives again, this time pulling her body halfway into the sinking car. She opens her eyes, but everything is black and she's screaming Julia's name, a scream only she can hear within her mind, a scream that sounds much like her own name underwater. Her ears, they pound with each heavy beat of her heart. She and the car are pulled lower and she's still *reaching reaching reaching* to no avail, her lungs hot and her head and eardrums pounding from the pressure—*how deep is this?* she wonders, remembering how she used to dive for coins at the bottom of her pool when she was seven or eight—and she pulls herself out of the car and pushes off, one kick, two kicks, and surfaces, gasping. *A third time, I must go a third time.*

(three, the magical number)

Steadying her nerves as best as she can, she takes in and lets out three heavy breaths, takes in another lungful of air, and dives.

One kick, two kicks, three kicks, a fourth, and she's at the car; she has to feel for it. Her eardrums want to pop, to implode, but she pulls herself completely inside the vehicle this time, calling out her name—*Julia / Yuliya*—one hand holding onto the steering wheel while the other reaches out like a tentacle in all directions. But no one is there to be found, to be saved, but herself. She fights the urge to open her mouth, to take in a mouthful of saltwater and begin her quick death, when her hand brushes something floating within the cabin. She instinctively grabs on and knows what it is: a picture frame.

Drowning, she thinks. *I'm drowning going to drown I'm drowning—*

She pulls herself out of the car and pushes off what feels like the hood—in which direction she doesn't know—and swims toward the less blackish of blacks. She expects panicked fingers to curl around her ankle at any moment, pulling her down into the depths, greedy hands frantically grabbing onto her, climbing her body, hand-over-hand—another's life sacrificed to preserve one's own.

I couldn't save her.

Yuliya kicks toward the surface, one hand still holding onto the damn picture frame for some reason, and she's forgotten to count her kicks this time but knows it must be six or seven or maybe—

Not going to make it not going to make it going to drown trying to save

(her)

myself. One, two, three—as long as I'm counting I'm alive—four, should be at the surface by now the moon there it is I see it kick to the moon.

Her hands break the surface and then her face, and she inhales not water but crisp night air, her heart beating like rapid machinegun fire and she's cold, so cold, although her lungs are set ablaze. Catching her breath, she leans back in the water and stairs up at the moon.

"The moon, there it is," she says. "I see it."

Sore noodle-like arms fan out beside her and help as she pumps her legs to get her moving. She floats on her back, her breath starting to return to normal. She looks at the place where the car used to be, and sees a white face floating on the surface of the water. And after a while her back hits the sand and the tide laps foamy water around her body.

Faceless, she holds the picture frame up to the moon, lifting her head ever so slightly and tilting the cheap thing at an angle to capture its light. The photo is of Julia and her father, standing on this exact beach. She laughs, knowing who she is now, remembering.

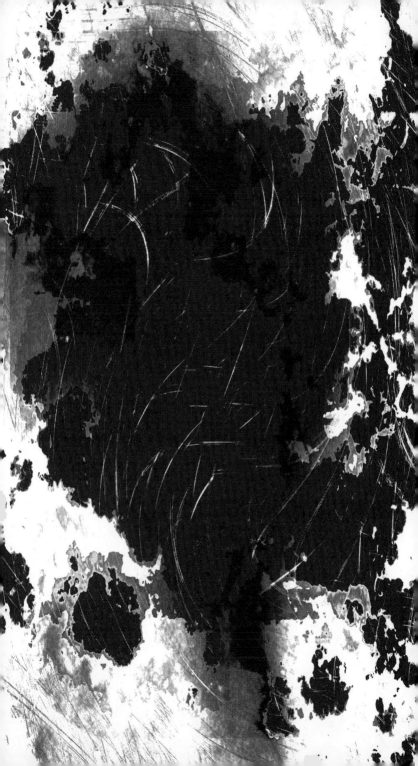

FADE TO BLACK

She was ten years old when the lake first swallowed her, the placid obsidian surface like an open mouth, and she'd been unable to swim, and so she fell deep into its hungry stomach.

Amber had been pushed—after backing down on a dare to jump in first—by one of the other girls at camp, either by her friend, Sarah, or her not-so-friend, Meghan. They didn't know she couldn't swim. *Amber* didn't know she couldn't swim, as she'd never tried anytime in her childhood; she always assumed she'd float, that buoyancy came naturally, that anyone could swim or else why had Mom and Dad never taken the time to teach her properly. Maybe Mom thought Dad taught her; maybe Dad thought the opposite; either way, they'd sent her far away to Loon Lake that summer because both had to work. It was Amber's first experience at a lake of any kind, and when the van pulled into the camp earlier that morning, she'd seen a group of girls her age splashing around, laughing. It had all looked so easy.

But it was long past dark when she and her friend and her not-so-friend snuck out of their shared tent to go night-swimming. They took with them nothing but flashlights and bathing suits, their towels and common sense left forgotten. They were breaking the rules and that was all that mattered at the time.

Three white flashlight beams sword-played in the darkness as wooden planks of the dock cried underneath their bare feet. They had giggled, as girls do when up to no good, shushing each other, holding arms to their chests in mock shivers, although the night was *anything* but cold. The lake, like any lake, Amber supposed, smelled like fish, like the duck ponds back home.

Eventually, three pairs of feet stood side-by-side-by-side at the edge of the water, which nearly lapped at their toes because of what Sarah called *the tides*.

The water was warm, and ever so inviting.

They dared each other for a while, a series of *you go first, no, you go firsts* and some innocent push-ing and even a failed *on the count of three we all jump in at once*. They shone their flashlights in the water, trying to see into its depths, but there seemed to be nothing below the surface but empty black. *I'm not scared, are you? Of course not. Are you?*

Looking down at the black was like looking at a giant spill of oil, the water as flat as glass. Three girls looked down upon three girls looking up— nearly a perfect mirror image with Amber in the middle—at a starlit sky both above and impossibly below, and the moon a luminous ball of light both floating in the sky and reflecting off the lake.

And then her arms were flailing and her feet slipping. She'd been pushed, a forceful smack against her back. At first she tried to turn, to see who'd done it, who'd pushed her, tried to grab at those arms to pull her—*or perhaps both of them*—into the water too, and at the last moment she turned back to the black wall and it slapped her in the face. She imagined their reflections shattering, the *whole world* shattering, as her head went under.

Amber tried to catch a breath but was too late and swallowed a mouthful of water that tasted the same as its stench: like fish, like algae, like duck pond. She spit something solid out of her mouth, like a piece of twig, but softer, something nasty. Completely submerged, her arms flailed like they had above water, but in the black water up was down and right was left and she was too afraid to open her eyes for what she might see. There was always something in the water because water attracted life. *There are living things down here*, she thought then, and would think forevermore, *and perhaps other things*. She could hear the girls' laughter, even underwater, like the warbling cackle of something long past dead.

She was thin, not yet starting to develop into womanhood—not a lot of meat on her fragile form—and so she sank, her body penciling straight down until pressure pierced her ears like the tips of sharpened pencils, and her feet touched soft ground. She tried to push off, but her toes sank deeper into the mush, through sucking mud, against slippery rocks, against slimy things. Her arms thrashed about, hoping perhaps to find the dock, but they found spindly-reaching plants and something that felt like a hand—*like fingers attached to a hand attached to an arm*—floating around her. Still, she couldn't open her eyes. She didn't *want* to open her eyes.

Deep underwater, her lungs burned. The laughing from her friend and not-so-friend above had started drowning-out, and then it was gone. Amber realized, for the first time in her entire life, that she could die. She could drown, actually *drown*, and die in this lake. No longer was she the invincible child, impervious to the rules of life and death like she'd always been; she was something fragile, not so permanent.

She kicked against soft mud and what felt like

spaghetti, tendrils of plant life—somehow growing underwater—able to wind around her legs, and then she felt the hand again, its clammy fingers wrapping around her ankle, and she screamed hard into the water.

Still, she couldn't open her eyes.

Amidst the bubbles of her trilled cry she heard something else in the lake, something *evil*, and she became still in order to listen. It was *laughter*, not the girls above, no, but something with her below, in the depths beneath the dock.

The hand at her leg let go—*a weed, a plant, a hand-like branch softened by prolonged submersion*—and for a moment Amber simply stayed motionless in the water, arms outstretched like a cross and feet as though nailed to it under the sludge holding her in place.

She *had* to open her eyes. She *had* to open her eyes. And she had to breathe. Someone was down there with her, watching her struggle. She could feel a presence, something female, something not alive. She *had* to open her eyes. She *had*—

Amber lifted her head skyward, surface-ward, and finally opened her eyes.

All was black but for the all-seeing moon looking upon her from above. The girls she'd come with to the lake so late at night were gone; they'd left her alone, to *die* alone, with the moon ominously watching over her instead.

The dead thing hiding under the dock continued to laugh, almost sweetly, like an eight- or nine-year-old girl, as if this dead child—this young *witch* already trapped beneath the water—would soon have a new friend to play with in the great what-ever-came-after-death, and she'd no longer be left alone, like Amber.

In a panic she kicked again, struggling to not give in and breathe in the black. One leg found purchase, pushing hard against a rock, the other still held captive. She kicked with her free foot, connecting with something that shifted, which made her look downward, at the countless glow-ing eyes staring back at her. Amber closed her own eyes, then, would keep them closed while underwa-ter from this point onward. *Rocks reflecting moonlight*, she told herself … *not eyes, rocks.* Her quickened pulse pounded in her ears, which throbbed. She squeezed her eyes shut, until they burned—like her chest, which felt at any second would implode or explode—and then she kicked with her free foot, at one of the eyes / rocks, and then both her feet were free.

Amber swam, or tried to because she didn't know how. She flopped her arms around, stroking the water as she'd seen people do, as she'd seen *dogs* do. The surface was so far away, she knew, and she felt like she was heading downward more than upward. She imagined the moon shrinking smaller, everything around her becoming dimmer.

She was not alone in the lake, where she'd die at only ten years of age. Her mouth opened like a fish, breathing water instead of air. Her arms paddled, but she spiraled round and round, or spherically— *up* once again becoming *down*, *left* becoming *right*.

The hand of whatever lived in the depths grabbed her ankle, wrapping tightly. Jagged fingernails dug into her skin, and she was pulled down / up until she met not the bottom of the lake, but the dock, her head hitting hard against it, her ears popping painfully. *How far down? How far down have I gone?* The water she breathed became air, and she coughed what didn't belong out of her lungs, retching onto the dock.

She had been *lifted* onto the dock.

"Open your eyes," someone had said to her, perhaps the witch, "open your eyes."

But she refused to open them, not for anyone, not even for herself.

Amber was helped into a sitting position and there she threw up an amount of putrid water that splashed against the wooden planks of the dock.

"You're okay," said a familiar voice, the camp counselor.

She was far from okay.

"Is she going to be all right?" said another familiar voice, her not-so-friend, Meghan, which meant Sarah was there too. They'd not left her alone to die, but had gone for help.

Still, she couldn't open her eyes, not until the following morning.

She was twenty years old when she took her first swimming lessons. After the traumatic experience at Loon Lake, she'd stopped going into open waters, stayed away from oceans, from swimming pools, even preferred showers over baths. She'd never learned to swim in all those years, despite nearly drowning. Around water, she was always wary, and so it took her another childhood lifetime to finally *take the plunge*, as she liked calling it— mostly to learn how to keep afloat if she ever fell into water accidentally.

Amber wasn't afraid of water—water attracted life, after all; and she wasn't afraid of what lurked beneath the water if she were to ever submerge again, because nothing was *really* there, only imaginings; she simply feared opening her eyes upon closing them, in case what she imagined ever became a reality.

As a child, she constantly had night terrors, with Mom or Dad often running into her room at ungodly hours of the morning to check on her. They'd look under her bed, examine her closet, assure her *nothing's there, sweetie, nothing's there*, although she'd remembered something being there:

the ghastly cackle, the reaching hand, those staring eyes.

It always started with a laugh and ended with a laugh, as far as she could remember. She'd finally grow tired from the strain of not sleeping—*don't fall asleep, don't fall asleep, don't fall asleep*, she'd chant—until her lids became heavy and her eyes closed on their own, and as she'd start to doze, she'd hear that childish, underwater laugh. *Eight or nine*, she'd tell herself. *The girl was / is eight or nine.* Mom and Dad, they'd rush in and find her sitting upright in bed with her eyes pressed closed, or covered by a bandana or part of her bed sheet. *You can open your eyes, sweetie*, they'd tell her, *it's safe*, and if she wore a covering they'd struggle with her to take it off. But it was never safe when she opened her eyes, *never*. Once, they'd told her those comforting words, and upon unmasking, the long-dead girl was next to her parents on the bed, smiling her crooked smile, decomposed hand reaching out. The only way to make her go away was to keep her eyes closed 'til morning. Yet she'd *feel* the girl—*the child witch*, Amber sometimes called her—still there, next to her on the bed. She'd feel the pressure of her weight on the mattress, smell her fishy reek. Long after her parents would leave, she'd hear them laughing too, through the walls.

She'll grow out of it, they'd say, *probably a phase.*

Sometimes they'd talk about therapy, how they

couldn't *afford* therapy.

Eventually, she'd find sleep, and she'd be fine until the following night. Sometimes she'd go as long as a week between terrors.

She'd throw a fit whenever her parents made her take a bath, which is why she now preferred showers. They'd tell her she wasn't using enough soap, that she needed suds, that a bath was pointless if she only sat in a tub of hot water. They never understood that sometimes, if she used bubble bath, or even shampoo or body wash for suds, she'd feel something under the foam, like stringy plants, like wiry hair, or that if she put her head underwater, she'd hear a warbled cackle coming from the drain, and sometimes, *sometimes*, she'd feel a hand around her stomach trying to hold her down, although she'd never fill the tub high enough to drown.

Amber liked the pools, though, after ten years avoiding them. She liked the shallowness and clarity, mostly, and the crowds of other swimmers—plenty of willing individuals to lend a hand if needed. She liked that the lap pool was only three feet deep in the beginner's area, that she could simply stand if anything were to happen, and she liked the life saver rings, which her instructor allowed her to use while practicing treading in deeper waters. Even in the deep end, she could see the blue bottom of the pool, and this was comforting.

But she'd never close her eyes. She wore goggles

to rid the sting of chlorine, or bromine, or whatever they put in the water, and along with treading, she learned four different strokes. Swimming became her therapy, and soon she could do it on her own, albeit always in crowds.

Whatever had haunted her since the incident at the lake stayed away from the pool. The little girl witch, if that's what she was, liked her to be alone.

Through college, Amber always had roommates coming and going, which helped, but they never stayed long. The night terrors eventually scared them off. By herself, in her dorm or shared apartment or wherever she found herself staying over the years, that's where she'd be haunted most. She learned to live with minimal sleep, with catnaps disturbed by laughter, or by the restraint of what became familiar hands. She knew that touch, *her* touch, and sometimes she'd wake with scratches on her skin, either self-inflicted or from her constant visitor, she didn't know. If anyone ever wrote a book about her, or a movie, they'd call it *The Girl with the Bags Under Her Eyes*, or perhaps *Skinny Girl*, because she rarely had an appetite.

The insomnia was maddening, and only made it worse, made the visits more frequent. She feared sleep. She feared the dark. And most of all, she not only feared closing her eyes, but *opening* them.

I could blind myself, she often thought. *I could sear my eyes, cut them out, sew my lids shut, blind myself. I could stare into the hot white sun until blind.*

But would it help? Would *not* seeing make it better, or worse?

She once held the tip of a pocket knife to her eye, staring at herself in the mirror for nearly an hour, her mind reeling, the blade shaking mere millimeters from the black of her pupil.

She sometimes wondered about cutting her wrists, how much courage / cowardice it would take to not only finish the first, but the second. How would such horrible symmetry even be possible? Always in front of a mirror, she contemplated these things, *always*—perhaps in hopes that her reflected self would talk her out of it. In either scenario, the hand with the weapon eventually pulled back, or *would be* pulled back, as if someone else were there.

It's you, she would tell the girl, or the empty room, *it's you keeping me from doing this to myself! Why? What do you want with me? I can do it*, she often told her mirrored self, or the girl, *I can get rid of you*, but she never could. Even if she managed one eye, one wrist, could she handle the other? How would the world look dark? *Will she stay with me when I die?*

Sometimes what you can't see, however, is more frightening than what you can, and so she could never bring herself to harm. She just couldn't do it, or wasn't allowed to do it.

The hesitation marks on her wrists eventually faded, as well as the temptations to blind herself, but the girl was always with her through the years, not aging *with* Amber, but trapped everlastingly at eight or nine years old.

There has to be a way out of this mess, she often told herself.

She was thirty years old when she found the nerve to face her fears, to return to Loon Lake. She was *there*, she knew—the dead girl, the *witch*, whatever she was, trapped under the docks. And so Amber allowed the lake to swallow her one last time, not with a friend and not-so-friend at her side to push her in, but alone and willingly. Because of the drought, the water had receded, with most of the remaining docks now old and dry and sun-bleached white like exposed bone. The much smaller brown surface of what remained of the lake was still an open mouth, yet smaller and parched and starved for too long—twenty years too long—and she had to walk farther out on the docks in order to find deep water, to find *her*. But she could swim this time, and so she didn't have to be pushed into its waters, into its hungry stomach.

As she remembered from her youth, the water stank of fish and filth, and there were actual ducks this time, a pair of female mallards, floating in the muck, beaks plunging for small fish and whatever creatures were attracted to the shallower warm water. They swam to her, wanting bread, and paddled off upon discovering she didn't have any.

She wore a swim suit, a two-piece this time, and a pair of goggles to protect her eyes, if only from the unclean water. She sat on the far end of the dock, cross-legged.

It took her most of the day to get into the water. She first dipped a toe, and then plunged her foot all the way to the ankle, and then the other foot, until she found herself sitting on the wooden planks with both feet completely submerged to her shins. And there she waited. And waited. What did she expect: hands to grab hold of her ankles, the familiar tingle of underwater plant life, the child-ish cackle? She closed her eyes, but neither felt nor heard any of these things.

I have to be in the water, she thought, *completely underwater.*

Amber grabbed the side of dock with both hands and lowered herself, up to her belly button. Her toes pointed downward, searching for the murky bottom, but even with the drought the waters were still deep at the end of this particular dock. *I dare you to go all the way in*, she could almost hear her childhood friend saying, *I dare you to close your eyes and go all the way in*. Sarah and Meghan, where were they now? Had they also been haunted? She lowered herself more, to the shoulders, her body posed like all those years ago: like a cross. Still, she couldn't touch the bottom. And then finally she took a deep breath, closed her eyes and mouth, and let go of the dock. She went under, almost completely, her body more buoyant than her ten-year-old self. She bobbed with her head above water, treaded lightly, and swam out a bit, although still close enough to the dock to reach out to it if necessary.

This was her first time swimming alone, and the thought of isolation so far from civilization was unnerving to the core. The water was warm, yet her skin prickled in goose flesh.

How far down does it go? she wondered, daring herself like her friends had all those years ago. *I bet you can't touch the bottom. I bet you're too scared …*

She kept her eyes open and penciled downward, her hands pushing the water as if trying to entice an audience. And she went down, and down, until finally her toes pushed through a soft layer of mud, and below that a layer of slimy rock. There was a small amount of pressure at her ears, but not like the sharp stabs she remembered feeling as a child. A few vine-like plants tickled her legs, and nothing more. Even with her eyes open, beneath the goggles, Amber could see only cloudy brown water. *What did you expect after disturbing the bottom of the lake?* She fanned her arms to keep her body below for a moment longer, and in doing so the back of her hand swiped what felt like aged bone, like a broken arm. *The dock*, she told herself, *it's only the dock.* She dared herself, like Sarah, like Meghan, to reach out, to close her eyes and touch the witch. Instead of a cackle, the only sound she heard underwater was her unsteady heartbeat, which beat synchronously in her ears, a soft yet rapid *thump-thump, thump-thump, thump-thump*. Her lungs began to burn, then—she had to go up soon for air—but she waited another dozen double-beats until her heart slowed, and reached out a hand.

It's her, the witch, she could almost hear her friends saying, beneath their stifled giggles, and for a moment it *was* her, until what felt like her fingers became a sunken branch, and what felt like the broken bones of her arm became a support beam holding up the dock, weathered to near dilapidation. When she surfaced, she almost retched, tasting the water on her lips, and she kicked away wispy hairs of whatever had tangled around her feet.

She went under, waited for the sediment to settle, and went under again, but nothing was there—not the girl, not her evil laugher. She scanned the surface below, looking for eyes—those staring eyes—but found only rocks, and pebbles, and mud.

She'll come at night, Amber told herself, and spent the rest of the afternoon sunbathing at the end of the dock, waiting for nightfall, for the stars and the moon. She waited until the water turned from brown to the obsidian black she remembered twenty years before.

Never had she felt so alone, but was she?

She's there, Amber knew. *Waiting all this time.*

Amber stayed until the moon shone directly over the lake, which also reflected at her feet. She stared down at herself staring back, as she had as a child. She imagined her childhood friend and not-so-friend on either side of her, backing away, too afraid to go on. The surface of Loon Lake had turned eerily placid, as flat as glass, as reflective as a mirror. *Black.*

Frogs and crickets played a strange harmony / melody until late into the night, and then suddenly stopped, as if reminding her that she was isolated, that it was finally time to close her eyes and go back into the water.

It took her even longer to dip her toes, and to sink her feet below the surface, and even longer to push out from the dock and submerge her body.

She shivered, even though the water felt warm. Night-swimming, she discovered, was something uncanny when done alone and in complete silence. She almost couldn't do it.

But I'm not alone. She's here with me, the girl.

After realizing her heart would never settle, Amber closed her eyes, knowing this was the only way she'd visit. She about-faced, toward the dock, where she'd been pushed into the water twenty years earlier.

This isn't right. I need to fall into the lake.

And so she reenacted the event, first pulling herself back onto the dock, and after a long hesitation, *falling* into the water, turning back toward where the two girls had stood, as if pushed, arms flailing, and at the last moment she turned to the black and it slapped her in the face. She went down, penciling to the bottom like before, memories flashing through her mind of weeds ensnaring her legs and mud sucking at her feet. Suddenly the memories became realities, and she found one of her bare feet stuck, the other slipping against a slimy rock, and her legs indeed became entangled. The back of a broken hand caressed her thigh, its touch soft and bloated. And she kept her eyes closed to all of it.

Open your eyes, said a voice other than her own. *Open your eyes.*

That was why she was here, after all, to *see*, but she still couldn't do it, couldn't pry open her eyes to see what had haunted her all these years. She pressed them closed until they burned. Her hand brushed against the dock, against the girl, and instantly her lungs were on fire. She gasped, taking in a mouthful of water and choked it out, her feet stuck, *really* stuck, and she felt the weeds about her feet wrapping tighter, tighter, the girl's fingers holding her down.

Open your eyes, the voice said again, muffled by the water, the gurgled sound erupting into something more like childish laughter.

Amber turned her head when the thing grabbed her, a pair of clawed hands cutting deep into each of her shoulders, but finally she opened her eyes, looking away from what held her down, away from the child witch. She looked instead to the rocks, which reflected moonlight, like open eyes, each staring at her. She kicked against the rocks, against the slippery eyes—*I need air I need air I need air*—until both her legs were freed yet still entangled, and her lungs, they'd soon implode or explode and fill—*I'm going to drown, stuck down here forever, like the girl, like the*—

She closed her eyes and faced her, prying off the goggles. If she were going to die, she at least had to *see* what had haunted her since first falling / pushed into the lake.

When she opened her eyes, the girl stared back with blinding light radiating from each glowing hole where her eyes should be, *deadlights*—around which she could see the burning silhouette of a girl of no more than eight or nine, her wispy hair and tiny form much like her own, as if she were staring at an outline of her youthful self, staring at a drowned version of herself beneath the water—and this light transformed her world from black to white.

Soon that was all she could see: *white*.

The weeds entangling her legs let loose, the fingernails holding her down instead wrapped around her waist, and although her mind spun her body round and round, Amber felt a sensation of rising toward the surface, the pressure at her ears lessening.

She could no longer see, even with her eyes pried wide, yet she heard the child one last time in her mind tell her to *open your eyes*—a *new* set of eyes, she knew, for they were already open—and when she impossibly opened them the white around her turned instantly black, and she couldn't help but gasp because it would be her final breath. Instead of water, she found air.

She'd been flung onto the dock, could feel it beneath her tired legs, and there Amber retched onto its old wooden planks.

Silence turned to night song, frogs and crickets recreating their harmony / melody. The sound of something like a girl splashed in the lake, in the darkness, and then the soft ripples in the water became nothing, like the fuzzy black that enveloped her.

Amber listened for the girl who'd saved her, but she was gone; she'd gone below.

She tried to open her eyes, but they were already that way.

She was forty years old and still blind, the dead girl from the lake no longer haunting her dreams, no longer there whenever she closed her eyes. Amber finally found decent sleep, although she listened for the girl each night before bed. And she'd wake each morning, no longer afraid to open her eyes, because opening them no longer served a purpose. But the lake was always hungry, and so she'd sometimes return there, albeit with help, with friends, and she'd swim in the black. She'd open her eyes under the water, always looking.

Also by Michael Bailey

Palindrome Hannah
[composite novel]

Scales and Petals
[fiction & poetry]

Phoenix Rose
[composite novel]

Inkblots and Blood Spots
[fiction & poetry]

Ensō
[children's fables]

Our Children, Our Teachers
[long fiction]

Oversight
[long / short fiction]

Forthcoming

Psychotropic Dragon
[composite novel]

The Impossible Weight of Life
[fiction & poetry]

Seen in Distant Stars
[novel]

Seven Minutes
[memoir]

Hangtown
[novel]

Prisms
[anthology, co-edited with Darren Speegle]

* Titles subject to change *

Edited Anthologies

Pellucid Lunacy

Chiral Mad

Chiral Mad 2

Qualia Nous

The Library of the Dead

Chiral Mad 3

You, Human

Adam's Ladder
[co-edited with Darren Speegle]

Chiral Mad 4: An Anthology of Collaborations
[co-edited with Lucy A. Snyder]

Miscreations: Gods, Monstrosities & Other Horrors
[co-edited with Doug Murano]

Made in the USA
Lexington, KY
09 December 2019